I

THE TALE OF
PETER RABBIT

彼得兔经典故事集
小兔彼得

[英]比阿特丽克斯·波特 著/绘　刘晓媛 刘懿 译

中国宇航出版社

·北京·

图书在版编目(CIP)数据

小兔彼得：英汉对照 /（英）波特(Potter,B.）著；
刘晓媛，刘懿译 . --北京：中国宇航出版社，2014.1
（2015.8重印）
（彼得兔经典故事集）
ISBN 978-7-5159-0555-6

Ⅰ. ①小… Ⅱ. ①波… ②刘… ③刘… Ⅲ. ①英语－
汉语－对照读物②童话－英国－近代 Ⅳ. ①H319.4：I

中国版本图书馆 CIP 数据核字（2013）第 280563 号

| 策划编辑 | 战　颖 | | 装帧设计 | 文道思 |
| 责任编辑 | 刘　杰　甄薇薇 | | 责任校对 | 战　颖 |

出　版
发　行　**中国宇航出版社**

社　址　北京市阜成路 8 号　　　　　邮　编　100830
　　　　（010）68768548
网　址　www.caphbook.com
经　销　新华书店
发行部　（010）68371900　　　　　（010）88530478（传真）
　　　　（010）68768541　　　　　（010）68767294（传真）
零售店　读者服务部　　　　　　　北京宇航文苑
　　　　（010）68371105　　　　　（010）62529336
承　印　北京画中画印刷有限公司
版　次　2014 年 1 月第 1 版　　　　2015 年 8 月第 5 次印刷
规　格　880×1230　　　　　　　开　本　1/40
印　张　3 ⅘　　　　　　　　　　字　数　104 千字
书　号　ISBN 978-7-5159-0555-6
定　价　29.80 元

前 言

　　亲爱的读者，您现在翻开的《彼得兔经典故事集》是一部畅销全球一百多年的经典之作，被奉为"世界绘本图书中不可高攀的顶峰"，是最温馨的亲子读物。在英语国家里，几乎每一个小孩都有过一两本波特的故事书。

作者简介

　　比阿特丽克斯·波特 (Beatrix Potter，1866—1943) 出生于英国伦敦一个富裕的家庭，父亲是位律师，热衷于艺术收藏和摄影。母亲很有艺术天分，尤其在水彩画上颇有造诣。波特的童年很孤独，她没有上过学，也没有玩伴，大部分时间，她都与弟弟在阴暗的家庭教室里度过。他们在教室里养了许多宠物，包括兔子、蝙蝠、刺猬、蜥蜴等。

　　从波特 5 岁起，他们一家人每年都会去佩斯郡的庄园里度假，那里激发了波特对自然科学的兴趣。其实波特小姐最初的理想是要成为一名研究真菌的科学家，无奈在她生活的时代，女性地位卑微，此类学科对女性的门槛非常高，于是她转而把对自然的热爱注入到绘画创作之中。

　　少女时代的的波特在弟弟的帮助下开始了职业插画师的生活。因自幼习画，且长期和大自然亲密接触，她非常擅长精细地描摹动植物的形态。她的画作超脱于当时的工业革命背景，全部以拟人的动物为主角，选取乡间生活为背景。

"彼得兔"系列图书令波特一举成名，荣誉也纷至沓来。但在未婚夫诺曼·沃恩因病去逝后，她离开了伦敦，回到她最初构思出"彼得兔"故事的英格兰湖区，开始了隐居创作、经营农场的生活。1913 年，47 岁的波特嫁给了乡村律师威廉·希利斯，婚后他们住在波特买下的农场里，守着一片美丽的湖水度过了 30 年。

"彼得兔"系列故事的诞生

1893 年，波特曾经的家庭教师的小儿子诺维尔生病了，她写信去安慰那个孩子。在长达八页的书信里，她第一个也是最著名的一个童话故事诞生了。她在信里写道："亲爱的诺维尔，我不知道应该给你写些什么，那么就让我给你讲一个关于四只小兔子的故事吧，他们的名字叫做——弗洛普茜、莫普茜、棉球尾与彼得……"1900 年，她从诺维尔那里把所有的信件都借回来，编成绘本，自费印刷了一批送给朋友们。由于反响不错，她下定决心要将这本绘本印刷出版。1902 年 10 月，在经历了多次失败之后，终于沃恩公司接受了"彼得兔"的故事。她也因此结识了出版商诺曼·沃恩，后来沃恩成为了她的未婚夫，从此开始了一段她与沃恩公司持续终生的友谊。

第一版的"彼得兔"印刷了 8000 本，这本图文并茂的童话书很畅销。到了圣诞节，这本书又被迅速地加印了 20000 本。波特从此成为了家喻户晓的名人。从 1902 年的《小兔彼得》到 1913 年的《小猪布兰德》，这 11 年间她出版了 20 多本绘本，这是她创作最为活跃的时期。婚后，波特曾一度搁笔。后来为了帮助陷入财务危机的沃恩家族，她又陆续出版了《阿普利·达普利的童谣》和《塞西莉·帕斯利的童谣》。

"彼得兔"系列故事共有 23 篇，先后被翻译成 36 种语言，在数十个国家出版发行，销量已超过千万册，被誉为儿童文学中的《圣经》。"彼得兔"的故事还被改编成芭蕾舞剧和动画片搬上舞台和荧屏，相关衍生产品，从海报、玩偶、纸牌游戏、婴儿毛毯到瓷器茶壶等也纷纷面世，久畅不衰。

本套"彼得兔"系列故事的特色

1. 根植于现实生活中的幻想。"彼得兔"是一部植根于人类生活环境中的动物童话，它对动物、植物的描绘都是以遵循自然规律为前提的，其描绘的精准性堪比科普读物。这种以自然科学常识为基础的幻想能带给孩子们科学与文学的双重娱乐。

2. 充满田园色彩的日常生活。在"彼得兔"系列故事中，几乎所有的故事都在田园背景下上演。美丽的原野、清澈的湖泊、茂密的森林、连绵的山谷、各种可爱的小动物……在这样一种宁静恬淡的背景之下，发生的故事也都亲切温馨，一如她清新淡雅的画风。

3. 全书充满了爱和美好。作者波特小姐穷极一生的心血营造出来一个小小的世界，她笔下的小动物形象全都是她饲养过、照料过的，她爱它们，并为它们写下了如此美好的文字。

4. 精美绝伦的插画散发着浓厚的纯真气息。波特小姐笔下的小动物们各具个性，形象动人，会让您不忍释卷，阅读本书会给您带来心灵休憩的愉悦。

5. 灵动、活泼的文字，将带给您极大的享受。中英对照的双语版本，加上优美的英文朗读，让您在听故事的同时，学习最美好的英文。

总之，"彼得兔"系列故事是西方公认的经典中的经典，那些既可爱又调皮的小动物们的形象，一个世纪以来一直受到人们的喜爱。孩子们喜欢这套书，因为它讲述的故事浅显易懂、插图栩栩如生，小动物们善良、单纯而可爱，动物之间发生的故事更是妙趣横生，令人忍俊不禁。成人们喜欢这套书，因为书中美丽的田园风光令人心驰神往，单纯的童话故事让心灵变得纯静，更因为它会让人想起自己的孩子们成长时的种种快乐与烦恼，这与书中动物妈妈们的快乐和烦恼是一样的。

全套系列图书收录的 23 篇童话各具异趣，字里行间洋溢着浓浓的友情和爱心。七百多幅精美的插画与温馨的文字相应成趣，会给读者带来极大的艺术享受。相信"彼得兔"系列故事会吸引每一位有童趣、有梦想的人阅读。

目录

1. The Tale of Peter Rabbit

小兔彼得

Once upon a time there were four little Rabbits, and their names were—Flopsy, Mopsy, Cotton-tail, and Peter.

They lived with their Mother in a sandbank, underneath the root of a very big fir-tree[1].

从前有四只小兔子，他们的名字分别是——弗洛普茜、莫普茜、棉球尾与彼得。

他们与妈妈一起住在一棵大杉树下的沙窝里。

"Now, my dears," said old Mrs. Rabbit one morning, "you may go into the fields or down the lane[2], but don't go into Mr. McGregor's garden."

"好了，我的孩子们，"一天早上，兔妈妈说，"你们可以去田野里玩，也可以去田间小路上玩，但是，不要走进麦格雷戈先生的菜园里。"

---

① fir-tree *n.* 杉树   ② lane *n.* 小路

"**Y**our Father had an accident there; he was put in a pie by Mrs. McGregor."

"你们的爸爸就是在那里出的事，他被麦格雷戈太太夹进了一张馅饼里。"

"**N**ow run along, and don't get into mischief①. I am going out."

"现在，去玩吧，不要淘气，我要出去一趟。"

① mischief *n.* 淘气

Then old Mrs. Rabbit took a basket and her umbrella, and went through the wood to the baker's. She bought a loaf of brown bread and five currant[①] buns.

然后，兔妈妈挎起篮子，拿上伞，穿过树林去面包房了。她买了一条黑面包和五块葡萄干小圆面包。

Flopsy, Mopsy, and Cotton-tail, who were good little bunnies, went down the lane to gather blackberries[②].

弗洛普茜、莫普茜和棉球尾都是乖巧的小兔子，他们沿着田间小路去摘黑莓了。

---

① currant *n.* 葡萄干

② blackberry *n.* 黑莓

4

But Peter, who was very naughty, ran straight away to Mr. McGregor's garden, and squeezed① under the gate!

但是彼得非常淘气，他径直跑向麦格雷戈先生的菜园，并从大门下面挤了进去。

---

① squeeze *v.* 挤

First he ate some lettuces① and some French beans②; and then he ate some radishes.

他先吃了一些莴苣和四季豆，然后，又吃了一些小萝卜。

And then, feeling rather sick, he went to look for some parsley③.

之后，他感到有些不舒服，于是开始去寻找西芹来消消食。

① lettuce *n.* 莴苣
② French bean 四季豆

③ parsley *n.* 西芹

6

But round the end of a cucumber① frame, whom should he meet but Mr. McGregor!

但是，绕到黄瓜架的尽头时，哎呀！他却遇到了麦格雷戈先生。

Mr. McGregor was on his hands and knees planting out young cabbages, but he jumped up and ran after Peter, waving a rake② and calling out, " Stop thief!"

麦格雷戈先生正半蹲在地上种小白菜，但是他一下子跳了起来，在后面追赶彼得，手中挥舞着耙子，叫喊着"捉贼！"

---

① cucumber *n.* 黄瓜

② rake *n.* 耙子

Peter was most dreadfully^① frightened; he rushed all over the garden, for he had forgotten the way back to the gate.

彼得吓得要死，他在菜园中乱窜，因为他已经忘记了通向大门口的路。

He lost one of his shoes among the cabbages,　and the other shoe amongst the potatoes.

他在白菜地里跑丢了一只鞋，在马铃薯地里跑丢了另一只鞋。

---

① dreadfully *adv.* 极其

After losing them, he ran on four legs and went faster, so that I think he might have got away altogether if he had not unfortunately run into a gooseberry[1] net, and got caught by the large buttons on his jacket. It was a blue jacket with brass[2] buttons, quite new.

弄丢鞋子之后，他用四条腿奔跑，跑得更快了。我认为，要不是他不幸撞到黑醋栗丛中的网上，夹克上的大纽扣被网挂住了，他或许早就逃脱了。他穿的是一件蓝色的夹克，上面有黄铜纽扣，还很新。

Peter gave himself up for lost, and shed[3] big tears; but his sobs[4] were overheard by some friendly sparrows, who flew to him in great excitement, and implored[5] him to exert himself.

彼得认为自己已经没有逃脱的希望了，于是他流下了大颗的眼泪。他的抽泣声被一群友善的麻雀无意中听到了，他们激动地飞到他面前，劝他要竭尽全力，争取逃脱。

① gooseberry *n.* 黑醋栗
② brass *n.* 黄铜
③ shed v. 流下

④ sob *n.* 啜泣
⑤ implore v. 恳求，哀求

Mr. McGregor came up with a sieve[1], which he intended to pop[2] upon the top of Peter; but Peter wriggled[3] out just in time, leaving his jacket behind him.

麦格雷戈先生拿着一只筛子赶过来，打算从彼得的头上突然扣下去，但是彼得及时地逃脱出来，只留下他的夹克。

And rushed into the tool-shed, and jumped into a can[4]. It would have been a beautiful thing to hide in, if it had not had so much water in it.

他仓皇地跑进工具房，跳进了一只喷壶中。如果喷壶里没有装那么多水，这里应该是一个完美的藏身之地。

---

① sieve *n.* 筛子
② pop *v.* 突然拿出
③ wriggle *v.* 摆脱
④ can *n.* 容器

Mr. McGregor was quite sure that Peter was somewhere in the tool-shed, perhaps hidden underneath a flower-pot. He began to turn them over carefully, looking under each.

Presently Peter sneezed[①]—"Kertyschoo!" Mr. McGregor was after him in no time.

麦格雷戈先生十分确信彼得就躲在工具房里的某个地方，或许藏在一只花盆下面。他开始小心翼翼地把花盆逐一翻过来，挨个查看着。

过了一会儿，彼得打了一个喷嚏——"阿嚏!"麦格雷戈先生立刻循声追了过去。

And tried to put his foot upon Peter, who jumped out of a window, upsetting[②] three plants. The window was too small for Mr. McGregor, and he was tired of running after Peter. He went back to his work.

他想要用脚踩住彼得，彼得却从窗口跳了出去，并撞翻了三棵植物。这个窗口对麦格雷戈先生来说太小了，而且他也厌烦了追赶彼得，于是回去干活儿了。

---

① sneeze v. 打喷嚏

② upset v. 打翻

Peter sat down to rest; he was out of breath and trembling[①] with fright, and he had not the least idea which way to go. Also he was very damp[②] with sitting in that can.

彼得坐下来休息休息，他喘得上气不接下气，吓得浑身发抖。应该走哪条路回去，他一点儿也没主意。同时，他也因为跳进了那只喷壶而浑身湿漉漉的。

After a time he began to wander about, going lippity—lippity—not very fast, and looking all round.

He found a door in a wall; but it was locked, and there was no room for a fat little rabbit to squeeze underneath.

过了一会儿，他开始四处徘徊，走起路来啪嗒——啪嗒地响——他走得不是很快，同时向周围张望着。

他发现墙上有一扇门，不过，门是锁着的，门下面没有缝隙，一只小肥兔是无论如何也挤不过去的。

---

① tremble *v.* 发抖

② damp *adj.* 潮湿的

An old mouse was running in and out over the stone doorstep, carrying peas and beans to her family in the wood. Peter asked her the way to the gate, but she had such a large pea in her mouth that she could not answer. She only shook[①] her head at him. Peter began to cry.

一只上了年岁的老鼠在石头门阶上跑进跑出，把豌豆与菜豆运回她树林里的家。彼得向她打听通往大门口的路，但是她嘴里叼着一颗大豌豆，无法回答彼得的问题。她只是冲彼得摇了摇头。彼得开始哭了起来。

---

① shook （shake的过去式）v. 摇头

$\mathbf{T}$hen he tried to find his way straight across the garden, but he became more and more puzzled. Presently, he came to a pond where Mr. McGregor filled his water-cans. A white cat was staring at some gold-fish; she sat very, very still, but now and then the tip of her tail twitched[①] as if it were alive.

Peter thought it best to go away without speaking to her; he had heard about cats from his cousin, little Benjamin Bunny.

然后，彼得想径直穿过菜园去找路，不过，他越走越困惑。过了一会儿，他来到了一个池塘边上，麦格雷戈先生就是在这里给喷壶灌水的。一只白猫正注视着池塘中的几条金鱼，她一动不动地坐在那里，只有尾巴梢偶尔抽动一下，仿佛它是活的。

彼得觉得最好赶快离开，别同她讲话。他曾听他的表兄小本杰明·邦尼说过许多猫的传闻。

① twitch v. 抽动，颤动

He went back towards the tool-shed, but suddenly, quite close to him, he heard the noise of a hoe①—scr-r-ritch, scratch, scratch, scritch. Peter scuttered② underneath the bushes.

彼得又向工具房走去，但是，突然，他听到了锄头的声音——咔哧，咔嚓，咔嚓，咔哧，这声音离他相当近。彼得急忙跑到一丛灌木下面，躲藏起来。

But presently, as nothing happened, he came out, and climbed upon a wheelbarrow③, and peeped over. The first thing he saw was Mr. McGregor hoeing onions. His back was turned towards Peter, and beyond him was the gate!

不过，等了一会儿，没有任何事情发生，他又钻了出来，爬上一辆独轮手推车，偷偷地窥视着。他最先看到的是麦格雷戈先生正在锄洋葱。他背对着彼得，而在他身边不远处就是大门口！

---

① hoe *n.* 锄头
② scutter *v.* 疾走

③ wheelbarrow *n.* 独轮手推车

Peter got down very quietly off the wheelbarrow, and started running as fast as he could go, along a straight walk behind some black-currant① bushes.

Mr. McGregor caught sight of② him at the corner, but Peter did not care. He slipped underneath the gate, and was safe at last in the wood outside the garden.

彼得悄悄地从独轮手推车上溜下来，沿着黑醋栗灌木丛后一条笔直的小路，开始拼命地奔跑起来。

麦格雷戈先生在拐角处发现了彼得，不过，彼得也顾不上那么多了。他从大门下面钻了出去，终于安全地跑进了树林里。

Mr. McGregor hung up the little jacket and the shoes for a scarecrow③ to frighten the blackbirds.

麦格雷戈先生把彼得的小夹克与鞋子挂起来，当成稻草人来恐吓黑鸟。

---

① black-currant *n.* 黑醋栗
② catch sight of 看见

③ scarecrow *n.* 稻草人

Peter never stopped running or looked behind him till he got home to the big fir-tree.

在跑到大杉树下家门口之前，彼得一直没有停下脚步，也没有回头看一眼。

He was so tired that he flopped^① down upon the nice soft sand on the floor of the rabbit-hole, and shut his eyes.

His mother was busy cooking; she wondered what he had done with his clothes. It was the second little jacket and pair of shoes that Peter had lost in a fortnight^②!

彼得累得筋疲力尽，扑通一声倒在兔子洞里柔软的沙地上，闭上了眼睛。

他的妈妈正在忙着做饭，她想知道彼得的衣服都到哪里去了。这是彼得在两个星期之内弄丢的第二件小夹克和第二双鞋了！

---

① flop *v.* 猛然坐下　　　　② fortnight *n.* 两星期

I am sorry to say that Peter was not very well during the evening.

His mother put him to bed, and made some camomile① tea; and she gave a dose of it to Peter!

"One table-spoonful to be taken at bed-time."

我要遗憾地告诉大家，那天晚上，彼得感觉很不舒服。

他的妈妈安排他躺在床上，并沏了一些甘菊茶。她让彼得喝了一剂甘菊茶！

"在睡觉前要喝上一大匙，病就好了。"

But Flopsy, Mopsy, and Cotton-tail had bread and milk and blackberries for supper.

但是，弗洛普茜、莫普茜与棉球尾在晚餐时却吃了面包、牛奶，还有黑莓呀。

---

① camomile *n.* 甘菊

2. The Tale of Benjamin Bunny

本杰明·邦尼

One morning a little rabbit sat on a bank.
He pricked[1] his ears and listened to the trit-trot, trit-trot of a pony.

A gig[2] was coming along the road; it was driven by Mr. McGregor, and beside him sat Mrs. McGregor in her best bonnet[3].

一天早上，一只小兔子坐在田埂上。

他竖起耳朵，听到小马踢踏、踢踏的脚步声。

一辆轻便的双轮马车沿着田野小路驶过来，马车是由麦格雷戈先生驾驶的，在他身边坐着麦格雷戈太太，戴着她最漂亮的帽子。

As soon as they had passed, little Benjamin Bunny slid down into the road, and set off—with a hop, skip, and a jump—to call upon his relations[4], who lived in the wood at the back of Mr. McGregor's garden.

马车刚一驶过去，小本杰明·邦尼就溜到了小路上，他兴高采烈、蹦蹦跳跳地去拜访他的亲戚们，他们就住在麦格雷戈先生家菜园后面的树林里。

---

① prick v. 竖起
② gig n. 双轮轻便马车
③ bonnet n. 无边女帽
④ relation n. 亲戚

That wood was full of rabbit-holes; and in the neatest, sandiest hole of all, lived Benjamin's aunt and his cousins—Flopsy, Mopsy, Cotton-tail, and Peter.

Old Mrs. Rabbit was a widow; she earned her living by knitting[1] rabbit-wool mittens[2] and muffetees[3] (I once bought a pair at a bazaar[4]). She also sold herbs, and rosemary[5] tea, and rabbit-tobacco (which is what we call lavender[6]).

那片树林里到处都是兔子洞，其中最整洁、沙子最多的洞里，住着本杰明的姑妈和他的表弟表妹们——弗洛普茜、莫普茜、棉球尾与彼得。

兔妈妈是一位寡妇，她靠编织兔毛连指手套和围巾为生（我曾经在一个集市上买了一副）。她也卖药草、迷迭香茶和兔烟草（这东西我们称之为薰衣草）。

---

① knit v. 编织
② mitten n. 连指手套
③ muffetee n. 围巾

④ bazaar n. 市场
⑤ rosemary n. 迷迭香
⑥ lavender n. 薰衣草

Little Benjamin did not very much want to see his Aunt.

He came round the back of the fir-tree, and nearly tumbled[①] upon the top of his Cousin Peter.

小本杰明不太想见他的姑妈。

他绕到了大杉树的后面，差一点儿撞到表弟彼得的脑袋。

Peter was sitting by himself. He looked poorly, and was dressed in a red cotton pocket-handkerchief[②].

"Peter,"—said little Benjamin, in a whisper—"who has got your clothes?"

彼得一个人坐在那里，看起来很可怜，他身上裹着一条红色的棉布围巾。

"彼得"，小本杰明轻声问，"谁拿走了你的衣服？"

---

① tumble *v.* 跌倒　　　　　② pocket-handkerchief *n.* 围巾

Peter replied—"The scarecrow in Mr. McGregor's garden," and described how he had been chased about the garden, and had dropped his shoes and coat.

Little Benjamin sat down beside his cousin, and assured[1] him that Mr. McGregor had gone out in a gig, and Mrs. McGregor also; and certainly for the day, because she was wearing her best bonnet.

彼得回答：“是麦格雷戈先生家菜园里的稻草人。”然后，他描述了自己如何在菜园里被追得到处跑，以至弄丢了鞋子与衣服的过程。

小本杰明在他表弟身边坐下来，向他保证麦格雷戈先生已经坐着一辆轻便的双轮马车离开了家，麦格雷戈太太也出了门，而且他们一定会在外面待一整天，因为麦格雷戈太太是戴着她最漂亮的帽子出去的。

———————
① assure v. 向……保证

Peter said he hoped that it would rain.

At this point, old Mrs. Rabbit's voice was heard inside the rabbit hole, calling—"Cotton-tail! Cotton-tail! fetch some more camomile!"

Peter said he thought he might feel better if he went for a walk.

彼得说希望天会忽然下起雨来，这样的话麦格雷戈太太的帽子就会被浇湿了。

就在这时，兔妈妈的声音从兔子洞中传来："棉球尾！棉球尾！再去采一些甘菊来！"

彼得说，如果能去散散步，他或许会感觉好一些。

They went away hand in hand, and got upon the flat top of the wall at the bottom of the wood. From here they looked down into Mr. McGregor's garden. Peter's coat and shoes were plainly[①] to be seen upon the scarecrow, topped with an old tam-o-shanter[②] of Mr. McGregor's.

他们手拉手离开，爬上了树林深处那堵墙的平坦的墙头。他们站在那里，俯视着麦格雷戈先生的菜园。他们清楚地看到彼得的外衣与鞋子正穿在稻草人的身上，而稻草人的头上则戴着麦格雷戈先生的一顶苏格兰旧便帽。

Little Benjamin said, "It spoils[③] people's clothes to squeeze under a gate; the proper way to get in, is to climb down a pear-tree."

Peter fell down head first; but it was of no consequence[④], as the bed below was newly raked and quite soft.

小本杰明说："从大门下面挤进去会弄坏衣服，进入菜园的正确方法，是从一棵梨树上爬下去。"

彼得头朝下摔了下去，不过，没有关系，因为下面的菜苗床刚被耙过，泥土还相当松软。

---

① plainly *adv.* 清楚地
② tam-o-shanter *n.* 苏格兰便帽
③ spoil *v.* 损坏
④ consequence *n.* 后果

It had been sown[1] with lettuces.

They left a great many odd little foot-marks all over the bed, especially little Benjamin, who was wearing clogs[2].

地里已经播下了莴苣的种子。

他们在地上留下了许许多多奇怪的小脚印，尤其是小本杰明，因为他穿着一双木底鞋。

---

① sown （sow的过去分词）v. 播种　　　② clog n. 木底鞋

Little Benjamin said that the first thing to be done was to get back Peter's clothes, in order that they might be able to use the pocket-handkerchief.

They took them off the scarecrow. There had been rain during the night; there was water in the shoes, and the coat was somewhat shrunk[①].

Benjamin tried on the tam-o-shanter, but it was too big for him.

小本杰明说，首先要做的事情是取回彼得的衣服，因为等会儿裹在彼得身上的那条围巾也许会派上别的用场。

他们把衣服和鞋从稻草人身上取了下来。由于夜晚下过雨，鞋子里面灌进了水，那件外衣也有点儿缩水。

小本杰明戴上了那顶苏格兰便帽，但是它对小本杰明来说实在太大了。

---

① shrunk （shrink 的过去式）v. 缩水

Then he suggested that they should fill the pocket-handkerchief with onions, as a little present for his Aunt.

Peter did not seem to be enjoying himself; he kept hearing noises.

然后小本杰明建议说，他们应该用那条围巾包些洋葱，作为送给姑妈的一份小礼物。

彼得似乎并不开心，他一直在倾听周围的声响。

Benjamin, on the contrary, was perfectly at home, and ate a lettuce leaf. He said that he was in the habit of coming to the garden with his father to get lettuces for their Sunday dinner.

(The name of little Benjamin's papa was old Mr. Benjamin Bunny.)

The lettuces certainly were very fine.

相反，小本杰明却非常自在，他还吃了一片莴苣叶子。他说他已经习惯了跟他父亲到这个菜园里来采摘莴苣，作为他们的周日大餐。

（小本杰明的父亲是老本杰明·邦尼先生。）

莴苣当然是非常美味的。

Peter did not eat anything; he said he should like to go home. Presently he dropped half the onions.

彼得什么都没有吃，他说他想要快点儿回家。不一会儿，他便掉落了一半的洋葱。

Little Benjamin said that it was not possible to get back up the pear tree, with a load of[1] vegetables. He led the way boldly[2] towards the other end of the garden. They went along a little walk on planks[3], under a sunny, red-brick wall.

The mice sat on their doorsteps cracking cherry-stones; they winked[4] at Peter Rabbit and little Benjamin Bunny.

小本杰明说，我们带着这么多蔬菜，不可能再爬上那棵梨树上返回了。他带路大胆地向着菜园的另一头走去。在阳光照耀下的红砖墙边，他们沿着一条厚木板铺成的小路走着。

几只老鼠坐在他们的门阶上面砸着樱桃核吃，他们向小兔彼得和小本杰明·邦尼眨着眼睛。

---

① a load of 很多
② boldly *adv.* 大胆地
③ plank *n.* 木板
④ wink *v.* 眨眼睛

Presently Peter let the pocket-handkerchief go again.

不久，彼得围巾里的洋葱又散落了一些。

They got amongst flower-pots, and frames and tubs. Peter heard noises worse than ever; his eyes were as big as lolly-pops[1]!

He was a step or two in front of his cousin, when he suddenly stopped.

他们走到摆放花盆、架子与木桶的地方。彼得听到了一些他从未听到过的可怕声音。他的眼睛瞪得像棒棒糖一样大！

他正走在他表哥前面一两步远的地方，他突然停下了脚步。

---

① lolly-pop *n.* 棒棒糖

This is what those little rabbits saw round that corner!

Little Benjamin took one look, and then, in half a minute less than no time, he hid himself and Peter and the onions underneath a large basket...

这就是两只小兔子在拐角处看到的景象！

小本杰明看了一眼，然后，立即把自己、彼得还有那些洋葱藏到了一只大篮子下面……

The cat got up and stretched[1] herself, and came and sniffed[2] at the basket.

Perhaps she liked the smell of onions!

Anyway, she sat down upon the top of the basket.

那只猫站了起来，伸了个懒腰，然后走到篮子旁边嗅来嗅去。

或许，她喜欢洋葱的味道！

不管什么原因，她坐在了那只篮子上，便不动了。

---

① stretch *v.* 伸展　　　　　② sniff *v.* 嗅

She sat there for five hours.

I cannot draw you a picture of Peter and Benjamin underneath the basket, because it was quite dark, and because the smell of onions was fearful[①]; it made Peter Rabbit and little Benjamin cry.

The sun got round behind the wood, and it was quite late in the afternoon; but still the cat sat upon the basket.

她在那里一连坐了五个小时，一动也不动。

我无法为你们画一张彼得与小本杰明藏在篮子下面的图画，因为那里太黑了。洋葱的味道实在太呛人了，小兔彼得与小本杰明都呛得流下了眼泪。

太阳落到了树林后面，已经是傍晚时分了，但是那只猫仍然坐在篮子上。

---

① fearful *adj.* 可怕的

At length there was a pitter-patter, pitter-patter, and some bits of mortar[1] fell from the wall above.

The cat looked up and saw old Mr. Benjamin Bunny prancing[2] along the top of the wall of the upper terrace[3].

He was smoking a pipe of rabbit-tobacco, and had a little switch[4] in his hand.

He was looking for his son.

到了后来，一阵噼哩啪哒、噼哩啪哒的声音传来，头顶的墙上落下来一些灰泥。

那只猫抬起头来，看到老本杰明·邦尼正沿着墙头昂首阔步地走过来。

他正叼着一根装有兔烟草的烟管，手中拿着一根软树枝。

他正在寻找他的儿子。

---

① mortar *n.* 砂浆
② prance *v.* 昂首阔步
③ terrace *n.* 台阶
④ switch *n.* 软枝条

34

Old Mr. Bunny had no opinion whatever of cats.

He took a tremendous① jump off the top of the wall on to the top of the cat, and cuffed② it off the basket, and kicked it into the green-house, scratching off a handful of fur.

The cat was too much surprised to scratch back.

老本杰明·邦尼对猫没有任何好感，一点儿也瞧不上它。

他在墙头上用力一跳，直接跳到了猫的头上，一巴掌把她从篮子上打了下去，直接一脚将她踢进温室里，还从她身上抓下一把猫毛。

那只猫惊呆了，完全忘记了如何反击。

When old Mr. Bunny had driven the cat into the green-house, he locked the door.

Then he came back to the basket and took out his son Benjamin by the ears, and whipped③ him with the little switch.

Then he took out his nephew Peter.

当老邦尼先生把那只猫赶进温室以后，他锁上了温室的门。

然后，他走回到篮子前，揪着儿子本杰明的耳朵，将他拖了出来，用那根软树枝抽打了他一顿。

然后，他把他的外甥彼得也拽了出来。

---

① tremendous *adj.* 极大的，巨大的
② cuff *v.* 拍，击

③ whip *v.* 抽打

Then he took out the handkerchief of onions, and marched out of the garden.

之后，他拖出了用围巾包裹的洋葱，他们三人列队离开了菜园。

When Mr. McGregor returned about half an hour later, he observed several things which perplexed[①] him.

It looked as though some person had been walking all over the garden in a pair of clogs—only the foot-marks were too ridiculously[②] little!

Also he could not understand how the cat could have managed to shut herself up inside the green-house, locking the door upon the outside.

半个小时以后，当麦格雷戈先生回来时，他发现了一些令他困惑不已的怪事。

似乎有人穿着一双木底鞋踏遍了他整个菜园——只是鞋印太小了，让人觉得莫名其妙！

同时，他也不能理解那只猫是如何将她自己关进温室并从外面锁上门的。

---

① perplex *v.* 困惑　　　　　　　② ridiculously *adv.* 荒谬地

When Peter got home, his mother forgave him, because she was so glad to see that he had found his shoes and coat. Cotton-tail and Peter folded up the pocket-handkerchief, and old Mrs. Rabbit strung① up the onions and hung them from the kitchen ceiling, with the bunches of herbs and the rabbit-tobacco.

当彼得回到家后，他的妈妈原谅了他，因为她很高兴地看到彼得找回了自己的鞋子与外衣。棉球尾与彼得把围巾叠了起来。兔妈妈则把洋葱串起来，并把它们与一束束药草和薰衣草一起挂在厨房的天花板上。

---

① strung （string的过去式） v. 用线串

3. The Tale of the Flopsy Bunnies

弗洛普茜·邦尼兔

It is said that the effect of eating too much lettuce is "soporific[1]".
I have never felt sleepy after eating lettuces; but then I am not a rabbit.
They certainly had a very soporific effect upon the Flopsy Bunnies!

据说，吃太多的莴苣，会昏昏欲睡的。

可我吃过莴苣之后，却从来没有过这种反应；但是话说回来，我又不是一只兔子。

但是莴苣对弗洛普茜·邦尼兔们有着非常强烈的催眠效果！

---

① soporific *adj.* 催眠的

When Benjamin Bunny grew up, he married his Cousin Flopsy. They had a large family, and they were very improvident[1] and cheerful.

I do not remember the separate names of their children; they were generally called the "Flopsy Bunnies".

当本杰明·邦尼长大以后，他娶了他的表妹弗洛普茜，他们组成了一个大家庭，过着简单舒适而又快乐无忧的生活。

我不记得他们每个孩子的名字，他们被通称为"弗洛普茜家的邦尼兔"。

As there was not always quite enough to eat—Benjamin used to borrow cabbages from Flopsy's brother, Peter Rabbit, who kept a nursery garden[2].

由于并不总是有足够多的食物可吃——本杰明经常向弗洛普茜的哥哥彼得兔借些圆白菜，因为彼得拥有一个苗圃。

---

① improvident *adj.* 无远见的   ② nursery garden 苗圃

Sometimes Peter Rabbit had no cabbages to spare.

有时候，彼得也没有多出来的圆白菜可借。

When this happened, the Flopsy Bunnies went across the field to a rubbish heap, in the ditch outside Mr. McGregor's garden.

当这种事情发生时，弗洛普茜家的邦尼兔们就穿过田野来到一个垃圾堆前找吃的，垃圾堆就在麦格雷戈先生花园外面的沟里。

Mr. McGregor's rubbish heap was a mixture. There were jam pots and paper bags, and mountains of chopped grass from the mowing machine (which always tasted oily), and some rotten vegetable marrows[1] and an old boot or two. One day—oh joy!—there were a quantity of overgrown[2] lettuces, which had "shot" into flower.

麦格雷戈先生的垃圾堆是一个大杂烩，这里有果酱罐、纸袋，割草机割下来堆积如山的碎草（它们总是有一种油腻腻的味道），一些腐烂的西葫芦和一两只旧靴子。有一天——噢，真让人兴奋！——这里长了一些枝繁叶茂的莴苣，它们都"开出"了花。

---

① vegetable marrow 西葫芦　　　　　② overgrown *adj.* 长得很快的

The Flopsy Bunnies simply stuffed lettuces. By degrees, one after another, they were overcome[①] with slumber[②], and lay down in the mown grass.

Benjamin was not so much overcome as his children. Before going to sleep he was sufficiently[③] wide awake to put a paper bag over his head to keep off the flies.

弗洛普茜家的邦尼兔们全都用莴苣填饱了肚子。慢慢地，他们一个接一个地被睡意征服了，躺倒在修剪过的草坪上。

本杰明没有像他的孩子们那样贪睡。在入睡之前，他还十分清醒地把一个纸袋套在他的脑袋上，以防止苍蝇接近，搅了他的美梦。

---

① overcome *v.* 征服，战胜
② slumber *n.* 睡意

③ sufficiently *adv.* 十分地

The little Flopsy Bunnies slept delightfully in the warm sun.

From the lawn beyond the garden came the distant clacketty sound of the mowing machine.

The blue-bottles[1] buzzed about the wall, and a little old mouse picked over the rubbish among the jam pots.

(I can tell you her name, she was called Thomasina Tittlemouse, a wood-mouse with a long tail.)

在温暖的阳光下，弗洛普茜家的邦尼兔们睡得酣畅淋漓。

从花园另一端的草坪上，传来割草机隐隐约约的轰鸣声。

青蝇们在墙头上闹哄哄地飞来飞去，一只上了年纪的小老鼠在果酱罐中翻找着垃圾，寻找着食物。

（我可以告诉你们她的名字，她叫小老鼠托马西娜，一只有着长尾巴的森林鼠。）

---

① blue-bottle *n.* 青蝇

She rustled across the paper bag, and awakened Benjamin Bunny.

The mouse apologized profusely[1], and said that she knew Peter Rabbit.

小老鼠爬过纸袋时发出了沙沙的响声，惊醒了本杰明·邦尼。

小老鼠不停地给本杰明·邦尼道歉，还说她认识彼得。

While she and Benjamin were talking, close under the wall, they heard a heavy tread above their heads; and suddenly Mr. McGregor emptied out a sackful of lawn mowings right upon the top of the sleeping Flopsy Bunnies! Benjamin shrank[2] down under his paper bag. The mouse hid in a jam pot.

当她与本杰明在离墙根很近的地方聊天时，他们听到头顶上传来了沉重的脚步声。突然间，麦格雷戈先生把一麻袋割下来的碎草倒了下来，正好倒在熟睡中的弗洛普茜家的邦尼兔们的身上！本杰明缩进了他的纸袋里，那只小老鼠藏进了一个果酱罐中。

---

① profusely *adv.* 毫不吝惜地
② shrank（shrink的过去式）*v.* 收缩

The little rabbits smiled sweetly in their sleep under the shower of grass; they did not awake because the lettuces had been so soporific.

They dreamt that their mother Flopsy was tucking them up[1] in a hay[2] bed.

Mr. McGregor looked down after emptying his sack. He saw some funny little brown tips of ears sticking up through the lawn mowings. He stared at them for some time.

睡梦中的小兔子们在鲜草的沐浴下甜甜地微笑着，他们没有醒过来，因为莴苣的催眠力量太强大了。

他们梦到他们的妈妈弗洛普茜把他们安置在一张干草床上并给他们盖上被子。

麦格雷戈先生把麻袋倒空以后，向下面俯视着。他看到一些有趣的褐色小耳朵尖从草堆中竖了出来。他盯着它们看了好一段时间。

① tuck up 盖好被子   ② hay *n.* 干草

Presently a fly settled on one of them and it moved.

Mr. McGregor climbed down on to the rubbish heap—

"One, two, three, four! five! six leetle rabbits!" said he as he dropped them into his sack. The Flopsy Bunnies dreamt that their mother was turning them over in bed. They stirred a little in their sleep, but still they did not wake up.

正在这时，一只苍蝇落在一只耳朵尖上，那只耳朵动了一下。

麦格雷戈先生马上从墙头爬下来，站到了那个垃圾堆上——

"一、二、三、四！五！六只小兔子！"他一边说，一边把小兔子们扔进他的麻袋里。弗洛普茜家的邦尼兔们梦到他们的妈妈正在床上帮他们翻身。他们在睡梦中翻动了一下，但是仍然没有醒过来。

Mr. McGregor tied up the sack and left it on the wall.

He went to put away the mowing machine.

麦格雷戈先生扎紧麻袋口，把麻袋放在围墙上。

然后他去收起割草机了。

While he was gone, Mrs. Flopsy Bunny (who had remained at home) came across the field.

She looked suspiciously at the sack and wondered where everybody was?

当麦格雷戈先生离开以后，弗洛普茜·邦尼太太（她仍然待在家中）穿越田野走过来。

她疑惑地打量着那个麻袋，心里感到很奇怪，其他人都到哪里去了呀！

Then the mouse came out of her jam pot, and Benjamin took the paper bag off his head, and they told the doleful[1] tale.

Benjamin and Flopsy were in despair, they could not undo the string.

But Mrs. Tittlemouse was a resourceful[2] person. She nibbled a hole in the bottom corner of the sack.

这时，那只小老鼠从她藏身的果酱罐中爬了出来，本杰明也把头顶的纸袋拿开，然后他们给邦尼太太讲述了刚刚那个悲惨的故事。

本杰明与弗洛普茜陷入到绝望之中，他们无法解开那根绳子。

但是，小老鼠太太是一个足智多谋的人。她在麻袋底部的一个角上一点一点地咬出了一个洞。

---

① doleful *adj.* 悲哀的　　　　② resourceful *adj.* 足智多谋

The little rabbits were pulled out and pinched[1] to wake them.

Their parents stuffed the empty sack with three rotten vegetable marrows, an old blacking-brush and two decayed turnips[2].

小兔子们被从麻袋里面拖了出来后，被掐醒了。

他们的父母把三个腐烂的西葫芦、一把旧的黑鞋刷和两个坏掉的萝卜装进了麻袋里。

Then they all hid under a bush and watched for Mr. McGregor.

然后，他们全都躲藏在一丛灌木下面，等候着麦格雷戈先生回来。

---

① pinch *v.* 掐，捏　　　　　② turnip *n.* 萝卜

Mr. McGregor came back and picked up the sack, and carried it off.

He carried it hanging down, as if it were rather heavy.

The Flopsy Bunnies followed at a safe distance.

麦格雷戈先生回来了，他拿起麻袋，提着它向远处走去。

麻袋在他手臂上垂了下来，似乎这麻袋相当沉重。

弗洛普茜家的邦尼兔们远远地跟在后面，与他保持着安全的距离。

They watched him go into his house. And then they crept up to the window to listen.

他们看着他走进房子里。

然后，他们蹑手蹑脚地走到窗户前去偷听。

Mr. McGregor threw down the sack on the stone floor in a way that would have been extremely painful to the Flopsy Bunnies, if they had happened to have been inside it.

They could hear him drag his chair on the flags, and chuckle—

"One, two, three, four, five, six leetle rabbits!" said Mr. McGregor.

麦格雷戈先生把麻袋重重地扔到石头地板上，如果弗洛普茜家的邦尼兔们还待在麻袋里面的话，这种扔法会把他们摔得非常疼痛的。

他们能够听到他在石头地板上拖着椅子，并且咯咯地笑着：

"一、二、三、四、五、六只小兔子！"麦格雷戈先生说着。

"Eh? What's that? What have they been spoiling now?" enquired Mrs. McGregor.

"One, two, three, four, five, six leetle fat rabbits!" repeated Mr. McGregor, counting on his fingers—"one, two, three—"

"Don't you be silly; what do you mean, you silly old man?"

"In the sack! one, two, three, four, five, six!" replied Mr. McGregor.

(The youngest Flopsy Bunny got upon the window-sill.)

"嗯？那是什么？他们现在又糟蹋什么了？"麦格雷戈太太询问道。

"一、二、三、四、五、六只小肥兔!"麦格雷戈先生重复着，数着他的手指，"一、二、三……"

"别犯傻了，你这是什么意思，你这个愚蠢的老头？"

"在麻袋里啊! 一、二、三、四、五、六!"麦格雷戈先生又重复了一遍。

（弗洛普茜家最小的邦尼兔爬上了窗台。）

Mrs. McGregor took hold of the sack and felt it. She said she could feel six, but they must be old rabbits, because they were so hard and all different shapes.

"Not fit to eat; but the skins will do fine to line my old cloak[①]."

"Line your old cloak?" shouted Mr. McGregor—"I shall sell them and buy myself baccy[②]!"

"Rabbit tobacco! I shall skin them and cut off their heads."

麦格雷戈太太抓住麻袋，摸了摸。她说她能感觉到里面确实有六个东西，不过，一定是六只老兔子，因为他们硬邦邦的，并且奇形怪状。

"他们不适合吃，不过他们的皮倒可以做我旧斗篷的衬里。"

"做你旧斗篷的衬里？"麦格雷戈先生嚷了起来，"我要把他们卖掉，给我自己买些烟草！"

"兔子烟草！我要剥他们的皮，砍掉他们的脑袋。"

---

① cloak *n.* 斗篷，披风　　　　　② baccy *n.* 烟草

Mrs. McGregor untied the sack and put her hand inside.

When she felt the vegetables she became very very angry. She said that Mr. McGregor had "done it a purpose".

麦格雷戈太太解开了麻袋，把她的手伸了进去。

当她发觉到里面是烂蔬菜时，她变得非常非常愤怒。她说麦格雷戈先生是"故意这么做的"。

And Mr. McGregor was very angry too. One of the rotten marrows came flying through the kitchen window, and hit the youngest Flopsy Bunny.

It was rather hurt.

麦格雷戈先生也非常生气。一只腐烂的西葫芦从厨房的窗户里飞出来，不偏不倚正好打中了那个最小的小兔。

这可是很痛的。

56

Then Benjamin and Flopsy thought that it was time to go home.

然后，本杰明与弗洛普茜觉得，应该是回家的时候了。

So Mr. McGregor did not get his tobacco, and Mrs. McGregor did not get her rabbit skins.

But next Christmas Thomasina Tittlemouse got a present of enough rabbit-wool to make herself a cloak and a hood, and a handsome muff① and a pair of warm mittens.

就这样，麦格雷戈先生没有得到他的烟草，麦格雷戈太太也没有得到她的兔皮。

不过，在第二年的圣诞节，小老鼠托马西娜却得到了相当多的兔毛，足够用来给她自己做一件斗篷、一块头巾、一副漂亮的皮手筒和一副温暖的手套。

① muff *n.* 皮手筒

4. The Story of a Fierce Bad Rabbit
一只凶猛的坏兔子

This is a fierce bad rabbit; look at his savage① whiskers,② and his claws and his turned-up tail.

这是一只凶猛的坏兔子。看看他野性的胡须、他的爪子和他向上翘起来的尾巴。

This is a nice gentle Rabbit. His mother has given him a carrot.

这是一只温顺的乖兔子。他的妈妈给了他一根胡萝卜。

The bad Rabbit would like some carrot.

坏兔子也想要一些胡萝卜。

---

① savage *adj.* 野性的，野蛮的　　　② whisker *n.* 胡须

He doesn't say "Please." He takes it!

他没有说"请给我"，他便抢走了胡萝卜。

And he scratches[1] the good Rabbit very badly.

　　并且，他还狠狠地抓伤了那只乖兔子。

The good Rabbit creeps[2] away, and hides in a hole. It feels sad.

　　乖兔子悄悄地爬走了，躲进一个洞里。他感到非常悲伤。

---

① scratch *v.* 抓，挠，刮　　　　　　② creep *v.* 爬行

This is a man with a gun.

这是一个带枪的男人。

He sees something sitting on a bench. He thinks it is a very funny bird!

他看到有什么东西坐在长椅上，他以为那是一个古怪的鸟！

He comes creeping up behind the trees.

他从树后面悄悄地走过去。

And then he shoots—BANG!

然后，他开枪了——砰！

This is what happens—

这就是发生的景象——

But this is all he finds on the bench[1], when he rushes up with his gun.

不过，当他拿着枪冲过去时，他在长椅上只看到了这些东西。

---

[1] bench *n.* 长凳

The good Rabbit peeps[①] out of its hole.

乖兔子从他的洞里偷偷地向外张望。

And it sees the bad Rabbit tearing past—without any tail or whiskers.

他看到坏兔子仓皇地逃走了——没有了尾巴，也没有了胡须。

---

① peep *v.* 偷看

5. The Tale of Mr. Tod

狐狸托德先生

I have made many books about well-behaved people. Now, for a change, I am going to make a story about two disagreeable① people, called Tommy Brock and Mr. Tod.

Nobody could call Mr. Tod "nice". The rabbits could not bear him; they could smell him half a mile off. He was of a wandering habit and he had foxy whiskers; they never knew where he would be next.

我已经写了很多本书了，写的都是行为端庄、彬彬有礼的小动物们。现在，我要改变一下，打算写两个讨人厌、招人烦的家伙，他们分别是獾子汤米和狐狸托德先生。

没有人说过托德先生的好话，兔子们无法忍受他，他们在半英里之外就能闻到他的气味。他留着狐狸式的胡须，习惯四处游荡，人们永远也不知道他下一次会出现在哪里。

---

① disagreeable *adj.* 不愉快的，讨厌的

One day he was living in a stick-house in the coppice①, causing terror② to the family of old Mr. Benjamin Bouncer. Next day he moved into a pollard③ willow near the lake, frightening the wild ducks and the water rats.

In winter and early spring he might generally be found in an earth amongst the rocks at the top of Bull Banks, under Oatmeal Crag④.

He had half a dozen houses, but he was seldom at home.

头一天，他会住在矮林中的柴屋里，让老本杰明·邦尼一家惶恐不安。第二天，他又会搬到湖边被修剪过的柳树林中，恐吓那些野鸭与河鼠。

在冬季与早春，通常会发现他待在一个岩石堆中的洞穴里，这个洞穴位于麦片峭壁下面的公牛堤上。

他有六座房子，但他很少待在家中。

---

① coppice *n.* 矮林
② terror *n.* 惶恐
③ pollard *n.* 被修剪的树木
④ crag *n.* 峭壁

The houses were not always empty when Mr. Tod moved out; because sometimes Tommy Brock moved in; (without asking leave).

Tommy Brock was a short bristly① fat waddling person with a grin②; he grinned all over his face. He was not nice in his habits. He ate wasp③ nests and frogs and worms; and he waddled about by moonlight, digging things up.

当托德先生外出时，这些房子也并不总是空着，因为有时候，獾子汤米未经允许就会住进去。

汤米是一只又矮又胖的獾子，他身上长满刚毛，走起路来摇摇摆摆，笑起来龇牙咧嘴。他满脸堆着笑，习性却不太好。他喜欢吃黄蜂的巢、青蛙与蠕虫，而且他总是在月光下蹒跚着四处游荡，喜欢挖一些东西出来。

---

① bristly *adj.* 长满刚毛的
② grin *n.* 咧嘴笑

③ wasp *n.* 黄蜂

His clothes were very dirty; and as he slept in the day-time, he always went to bed in his boots. And the bed which he went to bed in, was generally Mr. Tod's.

Now Tommy Brock did occasionally eat rabbit-pie; but it was only very little young ones occasionally, when other food was really scarce. He was friendly with old Mr. Bouncer; they agreed in disliking the wicked[1] otters[2] and Mr. Tod; they often talked over that painful subject.

他的衣服非常脏。他在白天睡觉时，总是穿着靴子上床，而他睡的床，通常是托德先生的。

獾子汤米偶尔会吃些兔子馅饼，不过，他只是在其他食物的确很短缺的情况下才偶尔吃非常小的兔子。他与老邦尼先生很友好，他们两个都讨厌邪恶的水獭和托德先生。他们经常谈论这个令人烦恼的话题。

---

① wicked *adj.* 邪恶的　　　　② otter *n.* 水獭

Old Mr. Bouncer was stricken in years. He sat in the spring sunshine outside the burrow[1], in a muffler[2]; smoking a pipe of rabbit-tobacco.

He lived with his son Benjamin Bunny and his daughter-in-law Flopsy, who had a young family. Old Mr. Bouncer was in charge of the family that afternoon, because Benjamin and Flopsy had gone out.

老邦尼先生年老多病，他坐在洞穴外面，沐浴着春日的阳光，他披着围巾，嘴里叼着一只装着兔烟草的烟斗。

他与儿子本杰明·邦尼、儿媳妇弗洛普茜住在一起，他们又有了一群小兔子宝宝。那天下午，本杰明与弗洛普茜外出去了，留下老邦尼先生看家。

The little rabbit babies were just old enough to open their blue eyes and kick. They lay in a fluffy[3] bed of rabbit wool and hay, in a shallow burrow, separate from the main rabbit-hole. To tell the truth—old Mr. Bouncer had forgotten them.

小兔宝宝们刚能睁开他们的蓝眼睛，蹬蹬小腿了。他们躺在铺满兔毛与干草的柔软的床上。他们的房间是一个浅洞，与大兔子洞隔开。说实话——老邦尼先生已经忘记他们了。

① burrow *n.* 洞穴
② muffler *n.* 围巾

③ fluffy *adj.* 蓬松的

He sat in the sun, and conversed cordially① with Tommy Brock, who was passing through the wood with a sack and a little spud② which he used for digging, and some mole③ traps. He complained bitterly about the scarcity④ of pheasants'⑤ eggs, and accused Mr. Tod of poaching⑥ them. And the otters had cleared off all the frogs while he was asleep in winter—

"I have not had a good square meal for a fortnight, I am living on pig-nuts⑦. I shall have to turn vegetarian⑧ and eat my own tail!" said Tommy Brock.

It was not much of a joke, but it tickled old Mr. Bouncer; because Tommy Brock was so fat and stumpy and grinning.

汤米正从树林里穿过，随身带着一个麻袋、一个挖东西的小锄头，还有一些鼹鼠夹。老邦尼坐在太阳底下，与獾子汤米热情地打了招呼。汤米愤愤不平地抱怨着野鸡蛋的短缺，指责托德先生窃取了它们。还有，水獭也趁他在冬眠时捕光了所有的青蛙：

"我已经两个星期没有吃上一顿像样的肉食了，我现在靠山核桃为生，我真应该变成素食主义者了，都吃我自己的尾巴啦！"獾子汤米说。

这句话本来没有什么好笑的，但是獾子汤米又胖又矮，一脸笑嘻嘻的样子却把老邦尼先生逗笑了。

---

① cordially *adv.* 热情地
② spud *n.* 小锄
③ mole *n.* 鼹鼠
④ scarcity *n.* 缺乏
⑤ pheasant *n.* 雉，野鸡
⑥ poach *v.* 窃取
⑦ pig-nut *n.* 山核桃
⑧ vegetarian *n.* 素食者

So old Mr. Bouncer laughed; and pressed Tommy Brock to come inside, to taste a slice of seed-cake and "a glass of my daughter Flopsy's cowslip[1] wine". Tommy Brock squeezed himself into the rabbit-hole with alacrity[2].

Then old Mr. Bouncer smoked another pipe, and gave Tommy Brock a cabbage leaf cigar which was so very strong that it made Tommy Brock grin more than ever; and the smoke filled the burrow. Old Mr. Bouncer coughed and laughed; and Tommy Brock puffed[3] and grinned.

And Mr. Bouncer laughed and coughed, and shut his eyes because of the cabbage smoke...

就这样，老邦尼先生放声大笑着，将獾子汤米推进洞中，请他品尝一片香籽饼，并对他说："喝一杯我儿媳弗洛普茜酿制的黄花九轮草葡萄酒吧。"獾子汤米灵巧地将自己的身体挤进了兔子洞。

然后，老邦尼先生又抽了一管烟，并递给汤米一只甘蓝叶雪茄，这只雪茄的劲儿相当大，这让獾子汤米笑得比以往更灿烂了。烟雾弥漫在洞穴中，老邦尼先生又是咳嗽又是笑；汤米也喷云吐雾，咧嘴笑着。

邦尼先生又是笑，又是咳嗽，一会便被甘蓝叶雪茄的烟雾熏得闭上了眼睛……

① cowslip *n.* 黄花九轮草
② alacrity *n.* 敏捷，灵活

③ puff *v.* 喷出

When Flopsy and Benjamin came back—old Mr. Bouncer woke up. Tommy Brock and all the young rabbit babies had disappeared!

Mr. Bouncer would not confess that he had admitted anybody into the rabbit-hole. But the smell of badger[1] was undeniable; and there were round heavy footmarks in the sand. He was in disgrace[2]; Flopsy wrung[3] his ears, and slapped[4] him.

Benjamin Bunny set off at once after Tommy Brock.

弗洛普茜与本杰明回来后——老邦尼先生才醒过来。獾子汤米与小兔宝宝们全都不见了！

老邦尼先生不承认他曾经让任何人进过兔子洞。不过，獾子的气味是无法否认的，并且沙地上有深深的圆脚印。他这下丢脸了，弗洛普茜揪着老邦尼的耳朵，责备着他。

本杰明·邦尼立刻出发去追赶獾子汤米。

① badger *n.* 獾
② in disgrace 丢脸
③ wring *v.* 拧
④ slap *v.* 责备

There was not much difficulty in tracking him; he had left his foot-mark and gone slowly up the winding footpath through the wood. Here he had rooted up the moss and wood sorrel[1]. There he had dug quite a deep hole for dog darnel[2]; and had set a mole trap.

A little stream crossed the way. Benjamin skipped lightly over dry-foot; the badger's heavy steps showed plainly in the mud.

The path led to a part of the thicket where the trees had been cleared; there were leafy oak stumps, and a sea of blue hyacinths[3]—but the smell that made Benjamin stop, was not the smell of flowers!

跟踪他并不难，他留下了脚印，因此可以看得出他沿着一条蜿蜒的小路缓慢地穿过树林。在这里，他把一些苔藓和酢浆草连根拔起；在那里，为了寻找犬毒麦，他挖了一个深洞，还放置了一个捕鼹鼠的夹子。

一条小溪横穿小路，本杰明轻盈地跳过去，连脚都没有湿，而那只獾子沉重的脚印却清清楚楚地印在了泥地上。

这条小路通向一片灌木丛，那里的树都被砍掉了，只剩下长着嫩叶的橡树桩和一片蓝色风信子的花海——然而，让本杰明停下脚步的味道，却不是花的香味！

---

① wood sorrel 酢浆草　　　　　　　　③ hyacinth *n.* 风信子
② darnel *n.* 毒麦

Mr. Tod's stick house was before him; and, for once, Mr. Tod was at home. There was not only a foxy flavour in proof of it—there was smoke coming out of the broken pail that served as a chimney.

Benjamin Bunny sat up, staring; his whiskers twitched[1]. Inside the stick house somebody dropped a plate, and said something. Benjamin stamped[2] his foot, and bolted[3].

He never stopped till he came to the other side of the wood. Apparently Tommy Brock had turned the same way. Upon the top of the wall, there were again the marks of badger; and some ravellings[4] of a sack had caught on a briar[5].

在他面前，是托德先生的柴屋！而这一次，托德先生待在家中。不仅有狐狸的气味可以为此作证——而且，那只破桶做成的烟囱里还飘出了缕缕轻烟。

本杰明·邦尼警觉起来，目不转睛地注视着，他的胡须在抽搐。在柴屋里面，有盘子摔碎的声音，还传来了说话声。本杰明跺了跺脚，撒腿就跑。

他一直到跑到树林的另一头才停下脚步。显然，獾子汤米也走了同一条路线。墙头上也留下了獾子的足迹，一棵石南树上还钩住几根麻袋的线头。

---

① twitch *v.* 抽动
② stamp *v.* 跺脚
③ bolt *v.* 逃跑
④ ravelling *n.* 碎片
⑤ briar *n.* 石南

Benjamin climbed over the wall, into a meadow[1]. He found another mole trap newly set; he was still upon the track of Tommy Brock.

It was getting late in the afternoon. Other rabbits were coming out to enjoy the evening air. One of them in a blue coat by himself, was busily hunting for dandelions[2]—"Cousin Peter! Peter Rabbit, Peter Rabbit!" shouted Benjamin Bunny.

The blue-coated rabbit sat up with pricked ears—

"Whatever is the matter, Cousin Benjamin? Is it a cat? or John Stoat[3] Ferret[4]?"

本杰明爬过围墙，来到一片牧场上。他发现了另一个新装的鼹鼠夹，看来他仍然跟在獾子汤米的后面。

现在已经将近黄昏了，其他的兔子们都从洞里钻出来，享受着傍晚的空气。其中一只穿着蓝色外衣的兔子，正在忙着找蒲公英——"彼得表弟！小兔彼得，小兔彼得！"本杰明·邦尼大声地叫喊着。

穿着蓝色外衣的兔子警觉地竖起了耳朵。

"怎么了，本杰明表哥？是看到猫了吗？还是看到白鼬约翰啦？"

---

① meadow *n.* 草地，牧场 　　③ stoat *n.* 白鼬
② dandelion *n.* 蒲公英 　　④ ferret *n.* 雪貂

"No, no, no! He's bagged my family—Tommy Brock—in a sack—have you seen him?"

"Tommy Brock? How many, Cousin Benjamin?"

"Seven, Cousin Peter, and all of them twins! Did he come this way? Please tell me quick!"

"不，不，不！是獾子汤米，他偷走了我的孩子——用一只麻袋装着——你看到他了吗？"

"獾子汤米？他偷走了几个孩子？本杰明表哥。"

"七个，彼得表弟，一胎生的所有孩子！他从这条路上过去了吗？请快告诉我！"

"Yes, yes; not ten minutes since ... he said they were caterpillars[1]; I did think they were kicking rather hard, for caterpillars."

"Which way? Which way has he gone, Cousin Peter?"

"He had a sack with something 'live in it; I watched him set a mole trap. Let me use my mind, Cousin Benjamin; tell me from the beginning." Benjamin did so.

"是的，是的，不到十分钟之前……他说麻袋里装的是毛毛虫。我当时还想，怎么可能是毛毛虫呢，它们踢得那么欢实。"

"哪条路，他走了哪条路，彼得表弟？"

"他拿了一个麻袋，里面装着些活蹦乱跳的东西。我看着他设置了一个鼹鼠夹。让我想一想，本杰明表哥，你把经过从头给我讲一遍。"于是本杰明把事情的经过说了一遍。

---

① caterpillar *n.* 毛毛虫

"My Uncle Bouncer has displayed a lamentable[1] want of discretion[2] for his years'" said Peter reflectively[3]; "but there are two hopeful circumstances. Your family is alive and kicking; and Tommy Brock has had refreshment[4]. He will probably go to sleep, and keep them for breakfast."

"Which way?"

"Cousin Benjamin, compose yourself. I know very well which way. Because Mr. Tod was at home in the stick house he has gone to Mr. Tod's other house, at the top of Bull Banks. I partly know, because he offered to leave any message at Sister Cotton-tail's; he said he would be passing." (Cotton-tail had married a black rabbit, and gone to live on the hill.)

"我的邦尼舅舅这些年来的判断力有所下降了，这真令人遗憾。"彼得若有所思地说，"不过，有两种现象表明还是有希望的：一是你的孩子们还活着，并且都活蹦乱跳的；二是獾子汤米已经吃过点心了。他有可能会睡上一觉，然后把小兔宝宝们留做明天的早餐。"

"他走的是哪一条路？"

"本杰明表哥，镇静一下，我非常清楚他走的是哪条路。既然托德先生待在柴屋中，那獾子一定去了托德的另一座房子，在公牛堤的上面。我知道一些情况，因为他愿意把任何消息都告诉我妹妹棉球尾，他说他会从那里经过的。"（棉球尾嫁给了一只黑兔子，搬到了那座小山上。）

---

① lamentable *adj.* 不快的
② discretion *n.* 判断力
③ reflectively *adv.* 沉思地
④ refreshment *n.* 点心

<big>P</big>eter hid his dandelions, and accompanied the afflicted① parent, who was all of a twitter. They crossed several fields and began to climb the hill; the tracks of Tommy Brock were plainly to be seen. He seemed to have put down the sack every dozen yards, to rest.

"He must be very puffed②; we are close behind him, by the scent③. What a nasty person!" said Peter.

彼得藏好了他的蒲公英，陪伴着这位痛苦的父亲一起去寻找孩子们。本杰明焦急得浑身颤抖不已。他们穿过了几片田野，开始爬那座小山。獾子汤米的足迹清晰可见，他似乎每走十几码就放下麻袋，休息一下。

"他一定已经气喘吁吁的了，从这些气味来判断，我们离他已经很近了。他真是一个讨厌的家伙！"彼得说。

---

① afflicted *adj.* 痛苦的　　　　　　　③ scent *n.* 气味
② puff *v.* 喘息

The sunshine was still warm and slanting[1] on the hill pastures. Half-way up, Cotton-tail was sitting in her doorway, with four or five half-grown little rabbits playing about her; one black and the others brown.

Cotton-tail had seen Tommy Brock passing in the distance. Asked whether her husband was at home she replied that Tommy Brock had rested twice while she watched him.

He had nodded, and pointed to the sack, and seemed doubled up with laughing—

"Come away, Peter; he will be cooking them; come quicker!" said Benjamin Bunny.

阳光仍旧很温暖，正斜照在山间的牧场上。在半山腰，棉球尾坐在自家门前，四五只半大的小兔子正在她身边嬉戏。其中一只小兔子是黑色的，其他几只是棕色的。

棉球尾刚才在远处看到獾子汤米走过去了。当询问到她的丈夫是否在家时，她回答说在她看着獾子汤米的那一会儿，她看到他休息了两次。

汤米点着头，指着麻袋，看起来好像高兴得笑弯了腰——

"走吧，彼得，他会吃了他们的，快点走！"本杰明·邦尼说。

---

① slant *v.* 倾斜

They climbed up and up—"He was at home; I saw his black ears peeping out of the hole."

"They live too near the rocks to quarrel with their neighbours. Come on, Cousin Benjamin!"

When they came near the wood at the top of Bull Banks, they went cautiously[①]. The trees grew amongst heaped[②] up rocks; and there, beneath a crag—Mr. Tod had made one of his homes. It was at the top of a steep bank; the rocks and bushes overhung it.

The rabbits crept up carefully, listening and peeping.

他们往山上爬啊爬——"他在家里，我看到他的黑耳朵从洞中探了出来。"

"他们住得离岩石堆太近，不能和他们的邻居吵架。走吧，本杰明表哥！"

当他们走进公牛堤上面的那片树林时，他们开始谨慎起来。树木从堆积的岩石中生长出来，在那里，在一个峭壁下面——托德先生为自己建造了一座房子。它位于一个陡峭堤岸的顶端，岩石与灌木垂悬在它的上面。

两只兔子小心翼翼地爬过去，仔细地聆听着，张望着。

---

① cautiously adv. 谨慎地　　　　② heap v. 堆积

This house was something between a cave, a prison, and a tumble-down[1] pig-stye. There was a strong door, which was shut and locked.

The setting sun made the window panes[2] glow like red flame; but the kitchen fire was not alight[3]. It was neatly laid with dry sticks, as the rabbits could see, when they peeped through the window.

Benjamin sighed with relief[4].

那幢房子像是洞穴，像是监狱，又像是一个摇摇欲坠的猪圈。它有一扇坚固的大门，大门紧闭并上了锁。

落日的余晖把窗玻璃映得像红色的火焰，不过，厨房里的柴火没有点燃。当两只兔子透过窗户向里面窥视时，可以看到厨房里整整齐齐地摆放着干柴。

本杰明如释重负般地出了一口气。

---

① tumble-down *adj.* 即将坍塌的
② pane *n.* 窗格
③ alight *adj.* 点着的
④ relief *n.* 宽慰

But there were preparations upon the kitchen table which made him shudder①. There was an immense② empty pie-dish of blue willow pattern, and a large carving knife and fork, and a chopper③.

At the other end of the table was a partly unfolded tablecloth, a plate, a tumbler④, a knife and fork, salt-cellar, mustard⑤ and a chair—in short, preparations for one person's supper.

不过，餐桌上已经准备好的一切，这又让本杰明颤抖起来。桌上放有一个绘有蓝色柳树图案的大空馅饼盘，还有用来切肉的大刀叉，以及一把砍刀。

在餐桌的另一端是一块半展开的桌布、一只盘子、一个平底玻璃杯、一副刀叉，还有盐瓶、芥末和一把椅子——总而言之，这都是为一个人的晚餐所做的准备。

---

① shudder *v.* 战栗，发抖
② immense *adj.* 巨大的
③ chopper *n.* 砍刀
④ tumbler *n.* 平底玻璃杯
⑤ mustard *n.* 芥末

No person was to be seen, and no young rabbits. The kitchen was empty and silent; the clock had run down. Peter and Benjamin flattened[1] their noses against the window, and stared into the dusk.

Then they scrambled round the rocks to the other side of the house. It was damp and smelly, and overgrown with thorns[2] and briars.

The rabbits shivered[3] in their shoes.

"Oh my poor rabbit babies! What a dreadful place; I shall never see them again!" sighed Benjamin.

看不到任何人，也看不到小兔子们。厨房里面空荡荡、静悄悄的，时钟也停摆了。彼得与本杰明把他们的鼻子紧贴在玻璃上，凝视着昏暗的厨房。

然后，他们绕过岩石堆，爬到房子的另一端。房子里潮湿，气味难闻，还生长着茂密的荆棘与石南。

两只兔子吓得腿直发抖。

"噢，我可怜的兔宝宝！多么可怕的地方啊，我再也见不到他们了！"本杰明叹口气说。

---

① flatten v. 使平坦
② thorn n. 荆棘

③ shiver v. 颤抖

They crept up to the bedroom window. It was closed and bolted[1] like the kitchen. But there were signs that this window had been recently open; the cobwebs[2] were disturbed, and there were fresh dirty footmarks upon the window-sill[3].

The room inside was so dark, that at first they could make out nothing; but they could hear a noise—a slow deep regular snoring grunt[4]. And as their eyes became accustomed to the darkness, they perceived that somebody was asleep on Mr. Tod's bed, curled up under the blanket—"He has gone to bed in his boots," whispered Peter.

　　他们爬上卧室的窗户，窗户关着并且上了插销，就像厨房一样。不过，有迹象表明，这扇窗户不久前刚被人打开过，因为上面的蜘蛛网被弄断了，窗台上还有刚刚留下的脏脚印。

　　房间里面非常昏暗，起初，他们什么也看不出来，不过，他们可以听到一个声音——缓慢、低沉而有规律的鼾声。当他们的眼睛习惯了黑暗以后，他们看出有个人正睡在托德先生的床上，身体蜷缩在毯子下面，彼得轻声说："他穿着靴子上了床。"

---

① bolt　*v.* 上门闩　　　　　　③ window-sill　*n.* 窗台
② cobweb　*n.* 蜘蛛网　　　　④ grunt　*n.* 呼噜声

Benjamin, who was all of a twitter, pulled Peter off the window-sill.

Tommy Brock's snores continued, grunty and regular from Mr. Tod's bed. Nothing could be seen of the young family.

The sun had set; an owl began to hoot[1] in the wood. There were many unpleasant things lying about, that had much better have been buried; rabbit bones and skulls[2], and chickens' legs and other horrors. It was a shocking place, and very dark.

They went back to the front of the house, and tried in every way to move the bolt of the kitchen window. They tried to push up a rusty nail between the window sashes[3]; but it was of no use, especially without a light.

浑身颤抖不已的本杰明把彼得从窗台上拉了下来。

獾子汤米的鼾声依然持续有规律地从托德先生的床上传来。但却仍看不到小兔子们的影子。

太阳落山了，猫头鹰开始在树林里鸣叫。四周有许多令人不安的东西，它们要是被埋起来就会好一些：有兔子的骨头与头盖骨，鸡腿以及其他让人感到恐怖的东西。这是一个令人毛骨悚然的地方，四周黑漆漆的一片。

他们回到房子前面，用尽了所有的办法想要移开厨房窗户上的插销。他们还试着撬起窗框之间一个生了锈的钉子。但是，没有用，尤其是在没有一丝光亮的情况下。

---

① hoot v. 发出鸣叫声　　　　　　　③ window sash 窗扇
② skull *n.* 头盖骨

They sat side by side outside the window, whispering and listening.

In half an hour the moon rose over the wood. It shone full and clear and cold, upon the house amongst the rocks, and in at the kitchen window. But alas, no little rabbit babies were to be seen!

他们肩并肩地坐在窗户外面，轻声交谈着，并侧耳聆听着。

半个小时之后，月亮升上树梢。它明亮、清澈而冰冷的光线照在岩石堆的那座房子上，也照在厨房的窗户上。不过，仍然看不到小兔宝宝们的影子！

The moonbeams twinkled on the carving knife and the pie-dish, and made a path of brightness across the dirty floor.

The light showed a little door in a wall beside the kitchen fireplace—a little iron door belonging to a brick oven, of that old-fashioned sort that used to be heated with faggots[1] of wood.

月亮的光芒在切肉刀和馅饼盘子上闪烁着，在肮脏的地板上映出了一条明亮的光路。

这片光芒正好照亮了厨房壁炉旁边的一扇小门——是用老式砖砌的烧木柴炉灶的一个小铁门。

---

[1] faggot *n.* 柴把，束薪

And presently at the same moment Peter and Benjamin noticed that whenever they shook the window—the little door opposite shook in answer. The young family were alive; shut up in the oven!

Benjamin was so excited that it was a mercy① he did not awake Tommy Brock, whose snores continued solemnly② in Mr. Tod's bed.

But there really was not very much comfort in the discovery. They could not open the window; and although the young family was alive—the little rabbits were quite incapable③ of letting themselves out; they were not old enough to crawl.

几乎与此同时，彼得与本杰明注意到，只要他们一晃动窗户——对面的那扇小门就会跟着晃动。原来那些小兔子们还活着，他们被关进了那个炉灶里！

本杰明激动万分，他没有吵醒獾子汤米真是侥幸，那只獾子仍在托德先生的床上怡然自得地打着鼾。

不过，这个发现并没有给他们带来多少宽慰。他们无法打开那扇窗户。尽管那些小兔子们还活着——但是他们太小了，没有能力自己逃出来，他们还不会爬。

---

① mercy *n.* 侥幸
② solemnly *adv.* 认真地
③ incapable *adj.* 不能的

After much whispering, Peter and Benjamin decided to dig a tunnel①. They began to burrow a yard or two lower down the bank. They hoped that they might be able to work between the large stones under the house; the kitchen floor was so dirty that it was impossible to say whether it was made of earth or flags.

They dug and dug for hours. They could not tunnel straight on account of stones; but by the end of the night they were under the kitchen floor. Benjamin was on his back, scratching upwards. Peter's claws were worn down; he was outside the tunnel, shuffling② sand away. He called out that it was morning—sunrise; and that the jays③ were making a noise down below in the woods.

窃窃私语了很久之后,彼得与本杰明决定挖一条地道。他们开始在堤岸下面一两码的地方挖掘,他们希望能够在房子下面的巨石之间挖出一条路来。厨房的地板太脏了,很难辨认它是泥土地还是石板地。

他们挖呀挖呀,挖了几个小时。由于沿途有岩石的缘故,他们不能笔直地往前挖掘。不过,天快亮的时候,他们挖到了厨房地板的下面。本杰明仰面躺在地上,向上挖着土。彼得的爪子都磨破了,他在地道外面把沙子运走。他大声说:"天已经亮了,太阳升起来了,松鸦们正在下面的树林吵吵嚷嚷"。

---

① tunnel *n.* 地道
② shuffle *v.* 搬移

③ jay *n.* 松鸦

Benjamin Bunny came out of the dark tunnel, shaking the sand from his ears; he cleaned his face with his paws. Every minute the sun shone warmer on the top of the hill. In the valley there was a sea of white mist, with golden tops of trees showing through.

Again from the fields down below in the mist there came the angry cry of a jay—followed by the sharp yelping bark of a fox!

Then those two rabbits lost their heads completely. They did the most foolish thing that they could have done. They rushed into their short new tunnel, and hid themselves at the top end of it, under Mr. Tod's kitchen floor.

本杰明·邦尼从黑暗的地道里爬了出来，把沙子从耳朵上抖落，用爪子擦了擦脸。随着时间一分一秒地过去，照在山顶上的阳光也变得越来越温暖。山谷里是一片白茫茫的雾海，金色的树梢显露出来。

山下弥漫着白雾的田野里再次传来一只松鸦愤怒的叫声——随后是一只狐狸的尖叫声！

这时，两只兔子完全失去了理智。他们干了一件有生以来最愚蠢的事情。他们冲进了新挖的短地道里，藏在了地道的尽头，就在托德先生厨房的地板下面。

Mr. Tod was coming up Bull Banks, and
he was in the very worst of tempers. First he
had been upset by breaking the plate. It was
his own fault; but it was a china plate, the
last of the dinner service① that had belonged
to his grandmother, old Vixen Tod. Then the
midges② had been very bad. And he had failed
to catch a hen pheasant③ on her nest; and it
had contained only five eggs, two of them
addled④. Mr. Tod had had an unsatisfactory
night.

托德先生走上了公牛堤，他的心情糟糕透顶。首先，他因打碎了那只盘
子而不高兴，这是完全他自己的错。但是，那是一只瓷盘，是他祖母老维克
森·托德那成套餐具中的最后一只了。此外，蚊虫的猖獗让他生气；还有，
他竟没能逮住一只正在孵蛋的野鸡，只找到了巢中的五只蛋，其中两只还是
坏的。托德先生过了一个不愉快的夜晚。

---

① dinner service 成套餐具
② midge *n.* 蚊

③ pheasant *n.* 野鸡
④ addle *v.* 腐坏

As usual, when out of humour, he determined to move house. First he tried the pollard willow, but it was damp; and the otters had left a dead fish near it. Mr. Tod likes nobody's leavings but his own.

He made his way up the hill; his temper was not improved by noticing unmistakable marks of badger. No one else grubs[①] up the moss so wantonly[②] as Tommy Brock.

像往常一样，当他心情不好时，他就决定搬家。起初，他去了被修剪过的柳树林中，不过，柳林中的房子太潮湿了，而且水獭们又在附近扔了一条死鱼。托德先生不喜欢任何人剩下的东西，除了他自己的。

他朝着山上走去，发现明显的獾的脚印后，他的心情没有任何好转。没有任何人会像獾子汤米那样无缘无故地挖掘苔藓。

---

① grub v. 挖掘　　　　　　　　　　② wantonly adv. 无缘无故地

Mr. Tod slapped his stick upon the earth and fumed[1]; he guessed where Tommy Brock had gone to. He was further annoyed by the jay bird which followed him persistently[2]. It flew from tree to tree and scolded, warning every rabbit within hearing that either a cat or a fox was coming up the plantation[3]. Once when it flew screaming over his head—Mr. Tod snapped at it, and barked.

He approached his house very carefully, with a large rusty key. He sniffed and his whiskers bristled[4]. The house was locked up, but Mr. Tod had his doubts whether it was empty. He turned the rusty key in the lock; the rabbits below could hear it. Mr. Tod opened the door cautiously and went in.

托德先生用手杖狠狠地敲着地面，怒气冲冲，他已经猜到了獾子汤米去了哪里。更令他恼火的是，那只松鸦一直不依不饶地跟在他后面，从一棵树上飞到另一棵树上，不停地斥责着他，并在听力可及的范围内警告着每一只兔子：不是猫就是狐狸正在朝着这个种植园走过来。有一次，当松鸦尖叫着飞过狐狸的头顶时——托德先生向他抓过去，大叫着。

他拿着一把生锈的大钥匙小心翼翼地走到自己的房子前。他用力嗅了嗅，胡子立刻竖了起来。房子虽锁上了，不过，托德先生怀疑里面有人。他在锁孔上转动着生锈的钥匙，地板下面的兔子听得清清楚楚。托德先生谨慎地打开门，走了进去。

---

① fume *v.* 发怒
② persistently *adv.* 坚持地

③ plantation *n.* 植物园
④ bristle *v.* 竖起

The sight that met Mr. Tod's eyes in Mr. Tod's kitchen made Mr. Tod furious①. There was Mr. Tod's chair, and Mr. Tod's pie-dish, and his knife and fork and mustard and salt-cellar and his tablecloth that he had left folded up in the dresser—all set out for supper (or breakfast)—without doubt for that odious② Tommy Brock.

There was a smell of fresh earth and dirty badger, which fortunately overpowered③ all smell of rabbit.

But what absorbed④ Mr. Tod's attention was a noise—a deep slow regular snoring grunting noise, coming from his own bed.

厨房的情景更是让托德先生火冒三丈。那是他的椅子，他的馅饼盘，他的刀叉、芥末、盐瓶，还有他叠好放在餐柜里的桌布——都被整整齐齐地摆了出来——毫无疑问，是獾子汤米那个讨厌的家伙为晚餐（或早餐）准备的。

幸运的是，新鲜的泥土味与臭烘烘的獾味，掩盖住了兔子的气味。

不过，吸引托德先生注意的是一个声音——从他床上传来的低沉、缓慢、有规律的鼾声。

---

① furious *adj.* 愤怒的
② odious *adj.* 可憎的，讨厌的
③ overpower *v.* 掩盖，压倒
④ absorb *v.* 吸引

He peeped through the hinges[1] of the half-open bedroom door. Then he turned and came out of the house in a hurry. His whiskers bristled and his coat-collar stood on end with rage[2].

For the next twenty minutes Mr. Tod kept creeping cautiously into the house, and retreating[3] hurriedly out again. By degrees he ventured further in—right into the bedroom. When he was outside the house, he scratched up the earth with fury. But when he was inside—he did not like the look of Tommy Brock's teeth.

He was lying on his back with his mouth open, grinning from ear to ear. He snored peacefully and regularly; but one eye was not perfectly shut.

他透过半敞开的卧室门铰链，向里面窥视了一下，然后转过身，匆忙地离开了他的房子。他的胡须直立着，愤怒地连衣领也立了起来。

在接下来的二十分钟里，托德先生不停地小心翼翼地爬进房子里，然后再匆忙地退出去。逐渐地，他试探地往前走着——直到完全进入卧室里。他在屋外面时，愤怒地刨着土。不过，当他进屋后——獾子汤米呲牙咧嘴的样子更让他生气。

獾子汤米仰面躺在床上，嘴巴大张着，像是笑得合不拢嘴。他平静而有规律地打着鼾，不过，有一只眼睛却没有完全闭上。

---

① hinge *n.* 铰链
② rage *n.* 愤怒

③ retreat *v.* 撤回

Mr. Tod came in and out of the bedroom. Twice he brought in his walking-stick, and once he brought in the coal-scuttle[1]. But he thought better of it, and took them away.

When he came back after removing the coal-scuttle, Tommy Brock was lying a little more sideways; but he seemed even sounder asleep. He was an incurably[2] indolent[3] person; he was not in the least afraid of Mr. Tod; he was simply too lazy and comfortable to move.

Mr. Tod came back yet again into the bedroom with a clothes line. He stood a minute watching Tommy Brock and listening attentively[4] to the snores. They were very loud indeed, but seemed quite natural.

托德先生在卧室里进进出出。有两次他把他的手杖拿了进来，还有一次他拿进来了一个煤筐。不过，他又想到了更好的主意，于是把它们都拿走了。

当他把煤筐拿走之后再进来时，獾子汤米身体稍微向旁边侧躺了一下。不过，他似乎睡得更熟了。他是一个懒得无可救药的家伙，他一点儿也不害怕托德先生，他只是太懒了，并且舒服得不想动弹。

托德先生拿着一根晾衣绳，再次回到卧室里。他站了一分钟，注视着獾子汤米并留神听着他的鼾声。那些鼾声的确非常响，不过，听上去十分自然。

---

① coal-scuttle *n.* 煤筐　　　　　③ indolent *adj.* 懒惰的
② incurably *adv.* 不可救药地　　④ attentively *adv.* 专心地

Mr. Tod turned his back towards the bed, and undid the window. It creaked; he turned round with a jump. Tommy Brock, who had opened one eye—shut it hastily. The snores continued.

Mr. Tod's proceedings[1] were peculiar, and rather uneasy, (because the bed was between the window and the door of the bedroom). He opened the window a little way, and pushed out the greater part of the clothes line on to the window-sill. The rest of the line, with a hook at the end, remained in his hand.

Tommy Brock snored conscientiously[2]. Mr. Tod stood and looked at him for a minute; then he left the room again.

托德先生转身背对着床，打开窗户。窗户发出了嘎吱的声音。他吃惊地跳转过身来，獾子汤米本来已经睁开的一只眼睛，此时又快速地闭上了，继续地打着鼾。

托德先生的行动很古怪，并且相当不安（因为那张床位于窗户与卧室的门之间）。他把窗户打开了一道缝，把晾衣绳的大部分推到外面的窗台上。绳子其余的部分，连同绳子末端的钩子，仍然握在他的手中。

獾子汤米还在装着认真地打着鼾，托德先生站在那里，看了他一会儿。然后，再次离开了房间。

---

① proceeding *n.* 行动　　　　② conscientiously *adv.* 认真地

Tommy Brock opened both eyes, and looked at the rope and grinned. There was a noise outside the window. Tommy Brock shut his eyes in a hurry.

Mr. Tod had gone out at the front door, and round to the back of the house. On the way, he stumbled[①] over the rabbit burrow. If he had had any idea who was inside it, he would have pulled them out quickly.

獾子汤米睁开双眼，看着绳子，咧嘴笑起来。窗外发出了一些声响，獾子汤米急忙又闭上眼睛。

托德先生从前门走出去，绕到了房子后面。在路上，他被那个兔子洞绊倒了。如果他知道谁藏在洞里面，他一定会马上把他们拖出来。

---

① stumble v. 绊脚

His foot went through the tunnel nearly upon the top of Peter Rabbit and Benjamin, but fortunately he thought that it was some more of Tommy Brock's work.

He took up the coil[①] of line from the sill, listened for a moment, and then tied the rope to a tree.

Tommy Brock watched him with one eye, through the window. He was puzzled.

他一脚踩塌了地道，差点儿踩到小兔彼得与本杰明的头上。不过，幸运的是，他认为这又是獾子汤米干的事。

他从窗台上拿起那卷绳子，侧耳倾听了片刻，然后把绳子系在一棵树上。

獾子汤米透过窗户用一只眼睛偷偷看着托德，他被搞糊涂了，不知道托德先生要干什么。

---

① coil *n.* 一卷

Mr. Tod fetched a large heavy pailful of water from the spring, and staggered[1] with it through the kitchen into his bedroom.

Tommy Brock snored industriously[2], with rather a snort.

Mr. Tod put down the pail beside the bed, took up the end of rope with the hook—hesitated, and looked at Tommy Brock. The snores were almost apoplectic[3]; but the grin was not quite so big.

Mr. Tod gingerly[4] mounted a chair by the head of the bedstead. His legs were dangerously near to Tommy Brock's teeth.

托德先生从山泉里打来满满一大桶水，拎着它摇摇晃晃地穿过厨房走进卧室。

獾子汤米仍在一丝不苟地打着鼾，还喷着鼻息。

托德先生把水桶放在床边，拿起绳子上带钩子的那一端——犹豫了一下，又看了看獾子汤米。獾子汤米的鼾声听起来几乎就像是得了中风。不过，他脸上的笑容却没有那么灿烂了。

托德先生小心翼翼地爬到床头的一张椅子上。他的腿差一点就挨上獾子汤米的牙齿了。

---

① stagger *v.* 摇晃
② industriously *adv.* 勤勉地

③ apoplectic *adj.* 中风的
④ gingerly *adv.* 小心翼翼地，谨慎地

He reached up and put the end of rope, with the hook, over the head of the tester① bed, where the curtains ought to hang.

(Mr. Tod's curtains were folded up, and put away, owing to the house being unoccupied. So was the counterpane②. Tommy Brock was covered with a blanket only.) Mr. Tod standing on the unsteady chair looked down upon him attentively; he really was a first prize sound sleeper!

It seemed as though nothing would waken him—not even the flapping rope across the bed.

他踮起脚尖往上够，把绳上带有钩子的一端绕到带华盖的床头上，那里应该是挂床帐的地方。

（托德先生的床帐已经折好放了起来，因为这座房子已经没人住了。床单也收了起来，因此獾子汤米只盖着一条毯子。）

托德先生站在摇摇晃晃的椅子上，专注地低头看着汤米，他可真能睡啊！

似乎没有什么声音能吵醒他——即使是绳子绕过床头发出的拍打声。

---

① tester *n.* 华盖，天盖　　　　② counterpane *n.* 床单

Mr. Tod descended safely from the chair, and endeavoured[1] to get up again with the pail of water. He intended to hang it from the hook, dangling[2] over the head of Tommy Brock, in order to make a sort of shower-bath, worked by a string, through the window.

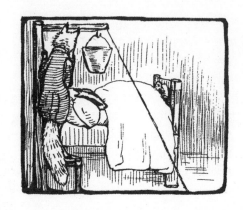

But naturally being a thin-legged person (though vindictive[3] and sandy whiskered)—he was quite unable to lift the heavy weight to the level of the hook and rope. He very nearly overbalanced himself.

The snores became more and more apoplectic. One of Tommy Brock's hind legs twitched under the blanket, but still he slept on peacefully.

托德先生安全地从椅子上下来，竭尽全力地提起那桶水，再次爬上椅子。他打算把水桶挂在钩子上，垂吊在獾子汤米的脑袋上方，这样只需要解开那根穿过窗户的绳子就可以给他洗个冷水浴。

不过，由于天生就四肢纤细（尽管有着强烈的报复心与沙子颜色的胡须）——把沉重的水桶举到与钩子和绳子一样的高度，确实有些为难他了。他几乎失去平衡了。

汤米的鼾声变得越来越像中风患者。他的一条后腿在毯子下面抽搐了一下，但他仍然尽量假装安静地睡着。

---

① endeavour *v.* 尽力，竭力　　　　　③ vindictive *adj.* 报复性的
② dangle *v.* 摇摆

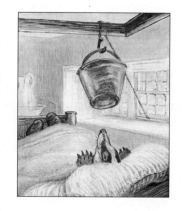

Mr. Tod and the pail descended from the chair without accident. After considerable thought, he emptied the water into a wash-basin and jug. The empty pail was not too heavy for him; he slung it up wobbling[①] over the head of Tommy Brock.

Surely there never was such a sleeper! Mr. Tod got up and down, down and up on the chair.

As he could not lift the whole pailful of water at once, he fetched a milk jug, and ladled[②] quarts of water into the pail by degrees. The pail got fuller and fuller, and swung[③] like a pendulum[④]. Occasionally a drop splashed over; but still Tommy Brock snored regularly and never moved—except in one eye.

托德先生安然无恙地拎着水桶从椅子上下来了。经过一番深思熟虑之后，他把水倒进了一只洗脸盆和一个水壶里。空桶对他来说就不算太沉了，他把空桶晃晃悠悠地挂在獾子汤米的脑袋上方。

的确，哪有过睡得这么深沉的人！托德先生在椅子上爬上爬下，爬下爬上，竟然没有吵醒他。

由于托德先生不能一下子举起满满一桶水挂上去，所以他取来了一个牛奶罐，用它把水一罐一罐地逐步舀进那只水桶里。水桶越装越满，摇晃着就像一个钟摆。偶尔有一两滴水溅出来，但是獾子汤米依然有规律地打着鼾，并且一动也不动——除了一只眼睛外。

---

① wobble v. 摇晃，摇摆
② ladle v. 以杓舀取
③ swang （swing的过去式）v. 摇摆
④ pendulum n. 钟摆

At last Mr. Tod's preparations were complete. The pail was full of water; the rope was tightly strained over the top of the bed, and across the window-sill to the tree outside.

"It will make a great mess in my bedroom; but I could never sleep in that bed again without a spring-cleaning of some sort," said Mr. Tod.

终于，托德先生完成了准备工作。水桶满满的，那根绳子的一端紧紧地系在床的上方，另一端穿过窗台系在窗外的树上。

"这下会把我的卧室弄得一团糟的。不过，如果不进行一次像春季大扫除那样的清扫，我是决不会再睡在这张床上的。"托德先生说。

Mr. Tod took a last look at the badger and softly left the room. He went out of the house, shutting the front door. The rabbits heard his footsteps over the tunnel.

He ran round behind the house, intending to undo the rope in order to let fall the pailful of water upon Tommy Brock—

"I will wake him up with an unpleasant surprise," said Mr. Tod.

托德先生最后看了一眼那只獾子，然后轻手轻脚地离开了卧室。他走到房子外面，关上了前门。两只兔子在地道里听到他的脚步声踏过。

他小跑着绕到房子后面，打算解开那根绳子，好让獾子汤米头顶那满满的一桶水落下来——

"我会用一个不令人愉快的突然袭击叫醒他。"托德先生说。

The moment he had gone, Tommy Brock got up in a hurry; he rolled Mr. Tod's dressing-gown[①] into a bundle, put it into the bed beneath the pail of water instead of himself, and left the room also—grinning immensely.

He went into the kitchen, lighted the fire and boiled the kettle; for the moment he did not trouble himself to cook the baby rabbits.

托德先生刚一离开，獾子汤米立刻从床上跳起来；他把托德先生的睡衣卷成一个卷儿，放在水桶下面的床上，用来代替自己接着躺在床上。然后他也离开了卧室——笑容灿烂地离开了。

他走进厨房里，点火烧起了水。此时，他没有心思去煮那些兔宝宝了。

---

① dressing-gown *n.* 睡衣

When Mr. Tod got to the tree, he found that the weight and strain had dragged the knot so tight that it was past untying. He was obliged to gnaw[①] it with his teeth. He chewed and gnawed for more than twenty minutes. At last the rope gave way with such a sudden jerk[②] that it nearly pulled his teeth out, and quite knocked him over backwards.

当托德先生来到那棵树前时，他发现重量与拉力已经让那个绳结打得死死的，无法解开了。他不得不用自己的牙齿去咬绳子。他又咬又啃，折腾了二十多分钟。最后，那根绳子被一股强烈的拉力绷断，这几乎把托德先生的牙齿也拽下来，还让他向后摔了一个跟头。

---

① gnaw *v.* 咬   ② jerk *n.* 猛拉

Inside the house there was a great crash and splash, and the noise of a pail rolling over and over.

But no screams. Mr. Tod was mystified[1]; he sat quite still, and listened attentively. Then he peeped in at the window. The water was dripping from the bed, the pail had rolled into a corner.

In the middle of the bed under the blanket, was a wet flattened something—much dinged[2] in, in the middle where the pail had caught it (as it were across the tummy). Its head was covered by the wet blanket and it was not snoring any longer.

从房子里面传来一声巨响和洒水的声音，接着是水桶滚来滚去的声音。

不过，没有尖叫声。托德先生很困惑，他静静地坐在那里，仔细地聆听着里面的动静。然后，他从窗口向屋内望去，水从床上滴到了地上，那只水桶已经滚到了一个角落里。

在床中央的毯子下面，是一个湿淋淋的、被压扁了的东西——中间被水桶击中的地方（似乎就在腹部）深深地凹陷了下去。那东西的脑袋被湿毯子盖住了，再也没有鼾声发出来了。

---

① mystified *adj.* 困惑的　　　　② ding *v.* 使受损

There was nothing stirring, and no sound except the drip, drop, drop drip of water trickling① from the mattress②.

Mr. Tod watched it for half an hour; his eyes glistened③.

Then he cut a caper④, and became so bold that he even tapped at the window; but the bundle never moved.

Yes—there was no doubt about it—it had turned out even better than he had planned; the pail had hit poor old Tommy Brock, and killed him dead!

没有任何嘈杂的响动，除了水从床垫上面滴滴答答落下来的声音以外，什么动静也没有。

托德先生观察了足有半个小时，他的眼睛开始闪闪发光。

然后，他欢呼雀跃起来，他变得肆无忌惮，甚至开始敲窗户。不过，那一卷东西仍然一动也不动。

对啦——这是毫无疑问的——这个结果比他计划的还要好。那个水桶砸中了可怜的老獾子汤米，直接送他归了西！

---

① trickle *v.* 滴下
② mattress *n.* 床垫
③ glisten *v.* 闪光
④ cut a caper 雀跃

"I will bury that nasty person in the hole which he has dug. I will bring my bedding out, and dry it in the sun," said Mr. Tod.

"I will wash the tablecloth and spread it on the grass in the sun to bleach[1]. And the blanket must be hung up in the wind; and the bed must be thoroughly disinfected[2], and aired with a warming-pan[3]; and warmed with a hot-water bottle[4]."

"I will get soft soap, and monkey soap, and all sorts of soap; and soda and scrubbing brushes[5]; and persian powder[6]; and carbolic to remove the smell. I must have a disinfecting. Perhaps I may have to burn sulphur[7]."

"我要把这个讨厌的家伙埋在他自己挖的洞里。我要把我的被褥搬到外面来，放在阳光底下晒干。"托德先生说。

"我要清洗桌布，把它晾晒在阳光下面的草地上漂白；再把毯子挂起来吹吹风；那张床必须彻底地消一下毒，然后用长柄暖床器通通风，再用热水袋焐一焐。"

"我要买软皂、猴子肥皂和各种肥皂，还要买苏打水、硬毛刷、杀虫粉和石碳酸来去除这个臭味。我必须消一下毒。或许，我还要烧些硫黄来熏一熏。"

---

① bleach *v.* 漂白
② disinfect *v.* 消毒
③ warming-pan *n.* 长柄暖床器
④ hot-water bottle 热水袋
⑤ scrubbing brush 硬毛刷
⑥ persian powder 杀虫粉
⑦ sulphur *n.* 硫黄

He hurried round the house to get a shovel from the kitchen—"First I will arrange the hole—then I will drag out that person in the blanket..."

He opened the door...

Tommy Brock was sitting at Mr. Tod's kitchen table, pouring out tea from Mr. Tod's tea-pot into Mr. Tod's tea-cup. He was quite dry himself and grinning; and he threw the cup of scalding[1] tea all over Mr. Tod.

他匆匆地绕过房子，去厨房里拿铁铲——"首先，我要处理一下这个洞——然后，我会把毯子里的那个家伙拖出来……"

他把门打开了……

獾子汤米坐在托德先生的餐桌前，正把茶从托德先生的茶壶里倒到托德先生的茶杯里。他的身上十分干爽，并咧嘴笑着。他把一杯滚烫的茶泼到了托德先生的身上。

---

① scald *v.* 烫伤

Then Mr. Tod rushed upon Tommy Brock, and Tommy Brock grappled[①] with Mr. Tod amongst the broken crockery[②], and there was a terrific battle all over the kitchen. To the rabbits underneath it sounded as if the floor would give way at each crash of falling furniture.

They crept out of their tunnel, and hung about amongst the rocks and bushes, listening anxiously.

接着，托德先生向獾子汤米冲过去，獾子汤米与托德先生在碎陶片间大打出手，这场可怕的打斗殃及了整个厨房。对躲在地板下面的两只兔子来说，每一件家具倒下来发出的声响，听起来都像是要把地板砸穿。

他们从地道里爬了出来，徘徊在岩石堆与灌木<u>丛</u>中间，焦急不安地聆听着。

---

① grapple *v.* 扭打　　　　　　　② crockery *n.* 陶器

Inside the house the racket was fearful. The rabbit babies in the oven woke up trembling; perhaps it was fortunate they were shut up inside.

Everything was upset except the kitchen table.

And everything was broken, except the mantelpiece[1] and the kitchen fender. The crockery was smashed to atoms[2].

房子里面扭打的喧嚣声非常可怕。砖灶里面的兔宝宝们都被惊醒了，吓得浑身颤抖着，或许，他们被关在砖灶里是一件幸运的事情呢。

除了餐桌，所有的东西都被打翻了。

除了壁炉台与壁炉炉围，所有东西都被摔碎了。陶器被摔成了粉碎的碎片。

---

① mantelpiece *n.* 壁炉台　　　　　② atom *n.* 微粒

114

The chairs were broken, and the window, and the clock fell with a crash, and there were handfuls of Mr. Tod's sandy whiskers.

The vases fell off the mantelpiece, the canisters[①] fell off the shelf; the kettle fell off the hob[②]. Tommy Brock put his foot in a jar of raspberry[③] jam.

And the boiling water out of the kettle fell upon the tail of Mr. Tod.

　　几只椅子被摔得散了架，窗玻璃与钟表稀里哗啦地碎了一地，此外，还有托德先生的一把褐色的胡须被扯掉了。

　　花瓶从壁炉台上掉下来，瓶瓶罐罐都从橱架上掉下来，水壶也从铁架上滚下来。獾子汤米的脚还踩进了一瓶覆盆子酱中。

　　滚烫的水从水壶里洒出来，浇到了托德先生的尾巴上。

---

① canister *n.* （放咖啡、茶叶、烟等的）小罐　　③ raspberry *n.* 覆盆子
② hob　*n.* 铁架

When the kettle fell, Tommy Brock, who was still grinning, happened to be uppermost[1]; and he rolled Mr. Tod over and over like a log, out at the door.

Then the snarling[2] and worrying went on outside; and they rolled over the bank, and down hill, bumping over the rocks. There will never be any love lost between Tommy Brock and Mr. Tod.

当水壶掉下来时，正咧着嘴笑的獾子汤米正巧压在托德先生的身上。他抱着托德先生滚啊滚啊，就像抱着一根圆木一样，一起滚出了门。

然后，纠缠与撕咬继续在房外进行着。他们滚过了堤岸，滚下了小山，撞到了岩石上。在獾子汤米与托德先生之间，友谊再也不复存在了。

---

① uppermost *adj.* 最上面的　　② snarl *v.* 缠结

As soon as the coast was clear, Peter Rabbit and Benjamin Bunny came out of the bushes—

"Now for it! Run in, Cousin Benjamin! Run in and get them! While I watch at the door."

But Benjamin was frightened—

"Oh; oh! they are coming back!"

"No they are not."

"Yes they are!"

"What dreadful bad language! I think they have fallen down the stone quarry①."

Still Benjamin hesitated, and Peter kept pushing him—

"Be quick, it's all right. Shut the oven door, Cousin Benjamin, so that he won't miss them."

当危险刚一过去，小兔彼得与本杰明·邦尼就从灌木丛中钻了出来——

"就趁现在！快跑进房子里去，本杰明表哥！快跑进去，把他们带出来！我会在门口把风。"

但是本杰明被吓坏了——

"噢，不！他们马上就会回来的！"

"不，他们不会的。"

"他们会的！"

"别说那些吓唬自己的话！我认为他们掉进了采石场中。"

本杰明仍然有些犹豫，但彼得一直推着他：

"快点儿，没关系。把炉灶门关上，本杰明表哥，这样汤米就不会想起那些小兔子来了。"

---

① quarry　n. 采石场

Decidedly there were lively doings in Mr. Tod's kitchen!

At home in the rabbit-hole, things had not been quite comfortable.

After quarrelling at supper, Flopsy and old Mr. Bouncer had passed a sleepless night, and quarrelled again at breakfast. Old Mr. Bouncer could no longer deny that he had invited company into the rabbit-hole; but he refused to reply to the questions and reproaches[1] of Flopsy. The day passed heavily.

毫无疑问，这边在托德先生的厨房里，有一出鲜活的救援戏在上演！

在兔子洞的家中，气氛也并不令人舒服。

晚餐时吵过一架之后，弗洛普茜与老邦尼先生度过了一个不眠之夜。第二天早上吃早餐时，两个人又争吵了起来。老邦尼先生不再否认他曾经邀请过外人进入兔子洞，但是，他拒绝回应弗洛普茜的追问，也不接受她的责备。这一天在沉重的气氛中度过。

---

① reproach *n.* 责备

Old Mr. Bouncer, very sulky[1], was huddled[2] up in a corner, barricaded[3] with a chair. Flopsy had taken away his pipe and hidden the tobacco. She had been having a complete turn out and spring-cleaning, to relieve her feelings. She had just finished. Old Mr. Bouncer, behind his chair, was wondering anxiously what she would do next.

老邦尼先生绷着脸，蜷缩在一个角落里，用一把椅子把自己挡在面前。弗洛普茜拿走了他的烟管，并把烟草藏了起来。为了转换心情，她还把家具都搬了出去，进行了一次彻彻底底的春季大扫除。她刚刚打扫完。躲在椅子后面的老邦尼先生开始焦虑地思考着，她下一步将会干什么。

---

① sulky *adj.* 绷着脸的；生闷气的
② huddle *v.* 蜷缩
③ barricade *v.* 设路障

In Mr. Tod's kitchen, amongst the wreckage[1], Benjamin Bunny picked his way to the oven nervously, through a thick cloud of dust. He opened the oven door, felt inside, and found something warm and wriggling. He lifted it out carefully, and rejoined Peter Rabbit.

"I've got them! Can we get away? Shall we hide, Cousin Peter?"

Peter pricked his ears; distant sounds of fighting still echoed in the wood.

在托德先生的厨房里，在一片狼藉之中，本杰明·邦尼穿过厚厚的灰尘，紧张地向炉灶走去。他打开了砖灶的门，在里面摸索着，然后触到了一团温暖的、扭动着的小东西。他把它小心翼翼地拿了出来，然后又回到小兔彼得的身边。

"我把他们救出来了！我们逃得掉吗？我们应该先藏起来吗，彼得表弟？"

彼得竖起耳朵听着，远处的厮打声仍在树林里回荡着。

Five minutes afterwards two breathless rabbits came scuttering[2] away down Bull Banks, half carrying half dragging a sack between them, bumpetty bump over the grass. They reached home safely and burst into the rabbit-hole.

五分钟之后，两只气喘吁吁的兔子飞快地从公牛堤上跑下来，两人半提半拖着一只麻袋，在草地上跌跌撞撞。他们安全地回到了家里，一下子钻进了兔子洞中。

---

① wreckage n. 残片

② scutter v. 疾走

Great was old Mr. Bouncer's relief and Flopsy's joy when Peter and Benjamin arrived in triumph with the young family. The rabbit-babies were rather tumbled and very hungry; they were fed and put to bed. They soon recovered.

A long new pipe and a fresh supply of rabbit-tobacco was presented to Mr. Bouncer. He was rather upon his dignity; but he accepted.

当彼得与本杰明成功地带着小兔宝宝们回到家里时，老邦尼先生如释重负，弗洛普茜欣喜若狂。兔宝宝们在地上东倒西歪，一个个饥肠辘辘。他们被喂得饱饱的，然后被放到了床上。他们很快就恢复了过来。

一根长长的新烟管和一些新鲜的兔烟草又交到了邦尼先生手中。虽然他非常注意自己的面子，但他还是接受了。

Old Mr. Bouncer was forgiven, and they all had dinner. Then Peter and Benjamin told their story—but they had not waited long enough to be able to tell the end of the battle between Tommy Brock and Mr. Tod.

老邦尼先生得到了原谅，他们所有人坐在一起共进晚餐。然后，彼得和本杰明讲述了他们的故事——但是，他们等待的时间不够长，所以还不知道獾子汤米与托德先生之间打斗的结果呢。

6. The Tale of Jemima Puddle-Duck

水坑鸭杰迈玛

What a funny sight it is to see a brood① of ducklings with a hen!

—Listen to the story of Jemima Puddle-duck, who was annoyed because the farmer's wife would not let her hatch② her own eggs.

看到一窝小鸭子和一只母鸡在一起，是一个多么有趣的场景啊！

听听水坑鸭杰迈玛的故事吧，她正因为农夫的妻子不让她自己孵蛋而恼火呢。

Her sister-in-law, Mrs. Rebeccah Puddle-duck, was perfectly willing to leave the hatching to some one else—"I have not the patience to sit on a nest for twenty-eight days; and no more have you, Jemima. You would let them go cold; you know you would!"

"I wish to hatch my own eggs; I will hatch them all by myself," quacked Jemima Puddle-duck.

她的弟媳——水坑鸭丽贝卡太太却很乐意把孵蛋任务留给别人去做，"我没耐心在窝里一连蹲上二十八天，你也不会有这份耐心，杰迈玛。你会让蛋变冷的，你知道你会的!"

"我希望把自己的蛋孵出来，我要亲自把它们孵出来。"水坑鸭杰迈玛嘎嘎地叫着说。

---

① brood n. 一窝，一群   ② hatch n. 孵

She tried to hide her eggs; but they were always found and carried off.

Jemima Puddle-duck became quite desperate. She determined to make a nest right away from the farm.

她想方设法藏起她的蛋，不过，它们总是能被人发现，并被拿走。

水坑鸭杰迈玛非常失望，她决定在远离农庄的地方做一个窝。

She set off on a fine spring afternoon along the cart-road that leads over the hill.

She was wearing a shawl[1] and a poke bonnet[2].

她在一个天气晴朗的春日午后出发了，沿着一条通往山顶的马车道向前走去。

她披着一条披肩，戴一顶宽边女帽。

---

① shawl *n.* 披肩

② poke bonnet 宽边女帽

When she reached the top of the hill, she saw a wood in the distance.

She thought that it looked a safe quiet spot.

当她抵达山顶时，她看到远处有一片树林。

她认为那看起来像是一个安全而宁静的地方。

Jemima Puddle-duck was not much in the habit of flying. She ran downhill a few yards flapping her shawl, and then she jumped off into the air.

虽然水坑鸭杰迈玛不习惯飞行，但她扇动着披肩，沿着小山向下跑了一段，随即跃到了半空中。

She flew beautifully when she had got a good start.

She skimmed along over[1] the tree-tops until she saw an open place in the middle of the wood, where the trees and brushwood had been cleared.

有了一个良好的开端，她姿势优美地飞行起来。

她掠过树林里的树梢，直到在树林中央看到一片开阔的地方，那里的树木与灌木丛都被清除掉了。

---

① skim over 掠过

Jemima alighted① rather heavily, and began to waddle② about in search of a convenient dry nesting-place. She rather fancied a tree-stump amongst some tall fox-gloves③.

But—seated upon the stump, she was startled to find an elegantly dressed gentleman reading a newspaper.

He had black prick ears and sandy-coloured whiskers.

"Quack?" said Jemima Puddle-duck, with her head and her bonnet on one side—"Quack?"

杰迈玛重重地落在地上，开始摇摇摆摆地寻找一个方便而干爽的地点做窝。她非常希望能在高高的毛地黄丛中找到一个树桩。

不过，她吃惊地看到了一位衣着优雅的绅士正在那个树桩上看报纸。

他长着黑色的尖耳朵和褐色的胡须。

"嘎嘎？"水坑鸭杰迈玛说，她的脑袋和宽边帽歪向一边，"嘎嘎？"

① alight v. 飞落
② waddle v. 摇摇摆摆地走

③ fox-glove n. 毛地黄

The gentleman raised his eyes above his newspaper and looked curiously at Jemima—

"Madam, have you lost your way?" said he. He had a long bushy[①] tail which he was sitting upon, as the stump was somewhat[②] damp.

Jemima thought him mighty civil[③] and handsome. She explained that she had not lost her way, but that she was trying to find a convenient dry nesting-place.

那位先生抬起头，眼睛越过报纸，好奇地打量着杰迈玛——

"夫人，你迷路了吗？"他问道。他长着一条毛茸茸的长尾巴，可能是那个树桩有些潮湿，他正坐在自己尾巴上。

杰迈玛心想他是一位多么有内涵而且相貌英俊的先生啊。她解释说她并没有迷路，不过，她想找一个方便而干爽的地点做窝。

---

① bushy *adj.* 蓬松的
② somewhat *adv.* 有点

③ civil *adj.* 有礼貌的

"**A**h! is that so? indeed!" said the gentleman with sandy whiskers, looking curiously at Jemima. He folded up the newspaper, and put it in his coat-tail① pocket.

Jemima complained of the superfluous② hen.

"Indeed? how interesting! I wish I could meet with that fowl③. I would teach it to mind its own business!"

"啊！是这样的吗？真的啊！"那位长着褐色胡须的先生问，好奇地看着杰迈玛。他把报纸折叠起来，放进燕尾服后摆的口袋里。

杰迈玛抱怨说那只母鸡太多余了。

"的确！太有意思了！我真希望能见见那只母鸡。我会教训她不要多管闲事的！"

---

① coat-tail *n.* 燕尾服
② superfluous *adj.* 多余的

③ fowl *n.* 母鸡

"But as to a nest—there is no difficulty: I have a sackful[1] of feathers in my wood-shed. No, my dear madam, you will be in nobody's way. You may sit there as long as you like," said the bushy long-tailed gentleman.

He led the way to a very retired[2], dismal[3]-looking house amongst the fox-gloves.

It was built of faggots[4] and turf[5], and there were two broken pails, one on top of another, by way of a chimney.

"不过，至于做窝嘛——没有问题，我的木棚里有一袋子羽毛。不，我亲爱的太太，你不碍任何人的事。你在那里可以想待多久就待多久。"那位长尾巴先生说。

他带着她来到毛地黄丛中一座非常偏僻，看起来有些阴暗的房子前。

这座房子是用柴捆和草皮建造起来的，在房顶有两只套在一起的破桶，用来当做烟囱。

---

① sackful *adj.* 一袋的
② retired *adj.* 隐蔽的
③ dismal *adj.* 阴暗的

④ faggot *n.* 柴捆
⑤ turf *n.* 草皮

"This is my summer residence[1]; you would not find my earth[2]—my winter house—so convenient," said the hospitable[3] gentleman.

There was a tumble-down[4] shed at the back of the house, made of old soap-boxes. The gentleman opened the door, and showed Jemima in.

那位热情好客的先生说："这是我夏天的住所，我冬天住的地方可没有如此便利。"

在房子后面有一个摇摇欲坠的小棚子，它是用旧肥皂盒搭建的。那位先生推开棚门，带杰迈玛走进去。

---

① residence *n.* 住所
② earth *n.* 洞穴
③ hospitable *adj.* 热情的
④ tumble-down *adj.* 摇摇欲坠的

The shed was almost quite full of feathers—it was almost suffocating①; but it was comfortable and very soft.

Jemima Puddle-duck was rather surprised to find such a vast quantity of feathers. But it was very comfortable; and she made a nest without any trouble at all.

那个棚子里几乎堆满了羽毛——虽说有些让人透不过气来，但是，却也非常舒适柔软。

水坑鸭杰迈玛看到如此多的羽毛非常吃惊。不过，这些羽毛非常舒适，于是她根本没费什么劲就为自己做了一个窝。

---

① suffocating *adj.* 令人窒息的，憋气的

When she came out, the sandy-whiskered gentleman was sitting on a log[①] reading the newspaper—at least he had it spread out, but he was looking over the top of it.

He was so polite, that he seemed almost sorry to let Jemima go home for the night. He promised to take great care of her nest until she came back again next day.

He said he loved eggs and ducklings; he should be proud to see a fine nestful in his wood-shed.

当杰迈玛走出棚子时，那个长着褐色胡须的先生正坐在一根圆木上读那张报纸——至少，他把报纸展开了，不过他的目光却在从报纸的上方向外瞟着。

他太彬彬有礼了，让杰迈玛回家过夜似乎都让他感到很难过。他答应好好照管杰迈玛的窝，直到她第二天再次回到这里。

他说他喜欢鸭蛋和小鸭子，看到他的木棚里有这么好的满满一窝小鸭子，他会感到很骄傲的。

---

① log *n.* 圆木

Jemima Puddle-duck came every afternoon; she laid[1] nine eggs in the nest. They were greeny[2] white and very large. The foxy gentleman admired them immensely. He used to turn them over and count them when Jemima was not there.

At last Jemima told him that she intended to begin to sit next day—"and I will bring a bag of corn with me, so that I need never leave my nest until the eggs are hatched. They might catch cold," said the conscientious[3] Jemima.

水坑鸭杰迈玛每天下午都会来小木棚看她的蛋；她在窝里下了九个蛋，蛋是浅绿色的，个头很大。那位狐狸模样的先生极其喜欢它们。当杰迈玛不在的时候，他总要过去把它们翻一翻，数一数。

最后，杰迈玛告诉他，她打算从第二天起开始孵蛋："我会带一口袋玉米过来，这样在蛋孵出来之前，我就不用离开我的窝了。否则它们会着凉的。"尽责的杰迈玛说。

---

① lay *v.* 下蛋
② greeny *adj.* 浅绿色的

③ conscientious *adj.* 尽责的

"**M**adam, I beg you not to trouble yourself with a bag; I will provide oats. But before you commence① your tedious② sitting, I intend to give you a treat. Let us have a dinner-party all to ourselves!"

"May I ask you to bring up some herbs from the farm-garden to make a savoury omelette③? Sage④ and thyme⑤, and mint and two onions, and some parsley⑥. I will provide lard⑦ for the stuff—lard for the omelette," said the hospitable gentleman with sandy whiskers.

"太太，请不必费心带玉米过来了，我会给你提供燕麦的。不过，在你开始乏味的孵蛋工作之前，我想要请你吃一顿大餐。让我们为自己举办一场宴会吧！"

"我能请你从农庄的花园里采一些香草过来做美味的煎蛋吗？再采些鼠尾草、百里香、薄荷、两头洋葱，还有一些西芹就好。我会给填料——给煎蛋——提供猪油。"那位长着褐色胡须、热情好客的先生说。

---

① commence *v.* 开始，着手
② tedious *adj.* 乏味的
③ omelette *n.* 煎蛋
④ sage *n.* 鼠尾草

⑤ thyme *n.* 百里香
⑥ parsley *n.* 西芹
⑦ lard *n.* 猪油

Jemima Puddle-duck was a simpleton[1]: not even the mention of sage and onions made her suspicious.

She went round the farm-garden, nibbling off snippets[2] of all the different sorts of herbs that are used for stuffing roast duck.

水坑鸭杰迈玛是个十足的笨蛋，甚至对鼠尾草与洋葱的提及都没让她产生怀疑。

她在菜园里转来转去，咬下了一片片不同种类用来做烤鸭的香料。

---

① simpleton *n.* 笨蛋，傻瓜　　　　　② snippet *n.* 小片

And she waddled into the kitchen, and got two onions out of a basket.

The collie-dog[1] Kep met her coming out, "What are you doing with those onions? Where do you go every afternoon by yourself, Jemima Puddle-duck?"

Jemima was rather in awe of[2] the collie; she told him the whole story.

The collie listened, with his wise head on one side; he grinned[3] when she described the polite gentleman with sandy whiskers.

然后，她摇摇摆摆地走进厨房，从一个篮子里拿了两头洋葱。

牧羊犬凯普在她出来时遇到了她。"你拿这些洋葱干什么？每天下午你都一个人去哪里了，水坑鸭杰迈玛？"

杰迈玛非常畏怯这只牧羊犬，她告诉了凯普整个故事的经过。

那只牧羊犬聆听着，聪明的脑袋歪向一边，听到杰迈玛描述那个彬彬有礼、长着褐色胡须的先生时，他咧嘴笑了起来。

---

① collie-dog *n.* 牧羊犬
② in awe of 对……畏怯

③ grin *v.* 咧嘴笑

He asked several questions about the wood, and about the exact position of the house and shed.

Then he went out, and trotted[1] down the village. He went to look for two fox-hound[2] puppies who were out at walk with the butcher.

他询问了几个关于那片树林的问题，还问了那座房子和那个棚子的确切地点。

然后他出了门，沿着村庄一路小跑。他去找跟着屠夫出去散步的那两只小猎狐犬了。

① trot *v.* 小跑   ② fox-hound *n.* 猎狐犬

Jemima Puddle-duck went up the cart-road for the last time, on a sunny afternoon. She was rather burdened[①] with bunches of herbs and two onions in a bag.

She flew over the wood, and alighted opposite the house of the bushy long-tailed gentleman.

在一个阳光明媚的下午，水坑鸭杰迈玛最后一次沿着马车道爬上小山。袋子里的几捆香草和两只洋葱让她脚步沉重。

她飞过树林，降落在那位长尾巴先生的房子对面。

---

① burden *v.* 负荷

He was sitting on a log; he sniffed the air, and kept glancing[1] uneasily[2] round the wood. When Jemima alighted he quite jumped.

"Come into the house as soon as you have looked at your eggs. Give me the herbs for the omelette. Be sharp!"

He was rather abrupt[3]. Jemima Puddle-duck had never heard him speak like that.

She felt surprised, and uncomfortable.

那位先生正坐在一根圆木桩子上，嗅着空气，不安地向树林四周张望。当杰迈玛落地时，他吓了一大跳。

"看完你的蛋就马上到房子里来。把煎蛋用的香草给我，快一点儿！"

他说话的态度相当粗鲁，水坑鸭杰迈玛从来没听到过他用这种语气说话。

她有些吃惊，并且很不自在。

---

① glance *v.* 扫视

② uneasily *adv.* 不安地

③ abrupt *adj.* 粗鲁的

While she was inside she heard pattering[1] feet round the back of the shed. Some one with a black nose sniffed at the bottom of the door, and then locked it.

Jemima became much alarmed[2].

她刚一走进棚子，就听到有急促的脚步声从棚子后面传来。一个长着黑鼻子的家伙在棚门底下嗅了嗅，然后锁上了棚门。

杰迈玛变得十分惊慌。

A moment afterwards there were most awful noises—barking, baying, growls and howls, squealing and groans.

And nothing more was ever seen of that foxy-whiskered gentleman.

接下来的片刻，外面传来可怕的声音——犬吠声、狗叫声、咆哮声、嗥叫声、尖叫声，还有呻吟声。

那位狐狸模样的先生再也没有人看到过。

---

① pattering *n.* 急促的轻拍声

② alarmed *adj.* 惊慌的

Presently Kep opened the door of the shed, and let out Jemima Puddle-duck.

Unfortunately the puppies rushed in and gobbled① up all the eggs before he could stop them.

He had a bite on his ear and both the puppies were limping②.

不一会儿，凯普打开棚门，让水坑鸭杰迈玛走出来。

不幸的是，那两只小猎狐犬却冲进了棚子里，在凯普还没来得及拦阻之前，吃掉了所有的鸭蛋。

凯普的耳朵上被咬了一口，那两只猎狗的腿也都一瘸一拐的。

Jemima Puddle-duck was escorted③ home in tears on account of those eggs.

水坑鸭杰迈玛被护送回了家。由于失去了那些蛋，她伤心地流下了眼泪。

---

① gobble *v.* 狼吞虎咽地吃
② limp *v.* 一瘸一拐

③ escort *v.* 护送

She laid some more in June, and she was permitted to keep them herself; but only four of them hatched.

Jemima Puddle-duck said that it was because of her nerves; but she had always been a bad sitter.

六月份的时候，她又下了一些蛋，这次她被允许自己孵蛋了。不过，只有四枚蛋孵出了小鸭子。

水坑鸭杰迈玛说，这是因为她太紧张的缘故。不过，她始终是一个不称职的妈妈。